"A cc

and a ... A truly enjoyable and impressive anthology."

—Tosca Lee, New York Times Bestselling author

"This collection presents a satisfying spectrum of storytellers, some familiar and others new on the scene. Some of the tales are unsettling and some are comforting; many are thought-provoking. Enjoy the ride."

—Kathy Tyers, author of the "*Firebird*" series, *Crystal Witness, Shivering World, One Mind's Eye*, and *Star Wars: The Truce at Bakura*

Praise for Mythic Orbits Volume 2

"A refreshingly unique and compelling collection. Raises the bar over the last Mythic Orbits, which I participated in. The stories both moved and delighted me. Truly mythic."

--Kerry Nietz, award-winning author of *Frayed* and *Amish Vampires in Space*.

Mythic Orbits
Volume 2

Best Speculative Fiction by Christian Authors

Table of Contents

Editor's Introduction

This anthology aims to collect the best available speculative fiction short stories written by Christian authors. That's whether the stories have openly Christian themes or characters or not, without requiring the stories to have any specific theme. (The anthology also limits itself to clean fiction—that is, no profanity, graphic sexuality or extreme violence.)

Over the past year, an online acquaintance questioned the purpose for the Mythic Orbits anthologies, stating that an anthology requires a unifying theme in order to succeed. To make sense and be marketable.

But there have been previous yearly anthologies based on the best science fiction and even fantasy from a given year (*World's Best Science Fiction,* edited by Donald A. Wollheim, *Terry Carr's Best Science Fiction of the Year* and *Terry Carr's Best Science Fiction and Fantasy of the Year*). So simply seeking the best available can be the goal of an anthology.

And anthologies can be organized around the writers as well, especially when there's something unusual about the category. For example, *Ciencia Ficción Argentina: Antología de*

Cuentos (Argentine Science Fiction: Anthology of Stories) was an anthology known by its authors—the nationality of the writers important because Argentinians are not widely-known to write science fiction.

So, is it widely-known all over the world that Christians write speculative fiction?

Well, clearly Christians who themselves are speculative fiction writers know what they write. But does everybody else?

Especially when we're talking about theologically conservative Christians, Evangelicals of some sort, professed Bible-believing Christians, do people know about their works? Is it legitimate for people to wonder if writers with personal convictions along these lines produce speculative fiction, that is, science fiction and fantasy and related genres like LitRPG, paranormal, and horror?

This book provides an answer: Not only do Christian writers produce speculative fiction stories, they write some great ones.

Enjoy these examples!

Travis Perry
Wichita Falls, TX
July, 2018

Living History

Steve Rzasa

Sam Iekel straightened his collar. He took a deep breath and let it out. Condensation obscured his reflection in the bathroom mirror. He wiped it away and was satisfied everything was perfect—blond hair slicked to one side, thick-rimmed glasses centered on bright blue eyes, white and red checkered shirt without wrinkles.

"You look great." Laura leaned around and kissed his cheek. She smelled floral, fresh from the sonic scrubber in the vestibule behind them.

"First days are always the worst." Sam's stomach grumbled, but his voice was steady.

"You'll be fine."

"Thanks."

Laura turned him around and held him at arm's length. She had olive skin and iridescent black hair. Her form-fitting gray jumpsuit was adorned with reflective orange stripes. A narrow diagnostic panel rippled lights along her left arm. "How's it fit?"

"The jeans itch."

"Genes? As in heredity?"

"No, j-e-a-n-s. The pants."

"Ah, I see." She wrinkled her nose. "They smell funny."

"It's cotton. Plant-based." Sam's heart hammered against his ribcage. "I'd feel better if this wasn't the third job in three months."

"Well, at least you won't have much competition for it. They need young humans."

"True."

"You can do this, Sam."

"As long as the Echoes agree." He clamped down on the negative thoughts and brought Laura in close for a kiss. "I love you."

"Love you, too."

Sam grabbed an antique messenger bag, faithfully replicated down to the last synthetic thread, and made sure all his equipment was present—laptop computer, tablet, and smartphone, the latter of which was synced to a smartwatch on his wrist. "See you after 1800 hours."

"I'll be done at Salvage Intake before that. Want me to pick up the rations?"

"Sure. I'll get them next week."

She blew him a kiss.

Sam donned a light fleece jacket and strapped the Vock to his neck. If any Echoes had trouble scanning him, he'd have to explain, and speaking Echo was impossible for most humans. The bronze device lined in black would handle translation. He opened the dorm hatch.

Sound assaulted him from all sides, a cacophony of voices intercut with quiet but incessant chirps. Their dorm was one of thousands in Resettlement Block Five stacked in long rows up and down this side of the orbital habitat. Walkways crisscrossed hazy green skies, ending in far-off platforms.

Fur and scales, carapaces and armored shells, even mechanical exoskeletons, surrounded him and the few hundred humans scattered throughout the lines. He met the gaze of an older woman, black hair shot through with silver, skin dark as coffee. Like everyone but Sam, she wore the same gray jumpsuit—same as Laura's, only striped green. Her Vock chirped softly. She nodded. He nodded back.

A thick-chested gurnx, tentacles dripping slime, shoved Sam hard. It slobbered words in a language he didn't understand, but the Vock it wore dutifully translated to Sam's unit: "Take your place, human."

No sense arguing. Sam stepped aside, letting the hulking being ahead. The woman across from him did likewise to a cii-chana floating in its life-support tank.

Your place.

Sam pushed the words from his mind as he watched the flat, round-edge transport drift down to receive passengers. He and all the other humans here learned where their place was, swiftly. It was behind other species.

Failure to comply meant relocation to Block Zero.

#

"Welcome to my neighborhood."

Sam spread his arms wide and smiled. He stood on a sidewalk in downtown Philadelphia on a sunny spring afternoon long extinct.

The smile was superfluous. His audience was entirely Echo. His historical research had dug up the term "blind as a bat." That prompted further inquiry into whatever a bat was, and he could see why it applied to the Echoes, who had no eyes, stubby snouts rounded into the rest of their faces, and two sets of wide, pointy ears. Their mouths were perpetually cracked part open, revealing hundreds of tiny translucent teeth. Short, covered in milky blue scales, and quadrupedal, they had four spindly limbs that bobbed as they walked.

"Today's March 10, 2017," Sam continued. "I'm on my way to work, so you're welcome to follow me. I'll show you around. Come on, guys."

He started down the sidewalk, stepping backwards, and made sure his earplugs were firmly in place. The vibration from the Echoes' constant probing their surroundings would give him a headache by the end of the day if he didn't.

There were thirteen in the group, typical brood size. Two were adult herders, taller than the rest by a foot but still topping out only at Sam's shoulders. The rest of the brood stayed around them, clustered in the hereditary arrangement for safety—tallest at four points, shorter inward.

One of them let out a sharp bark that rippled through the air, so intense Sam swore he could feel the sound pulse on his skin. [Is that a transport?]

Sam's Vock rendered it in halting, electronic English delivered through his earplugs. "Yes, it's an automobile."

[Auto-mobile. Is it autonomous?]

"No, people like me drive it. It's a car."

[Where is its propulsion?]

Sam opened the door. The smell of freshly-fabricated plastics and new paint washed over him. "Under the hood."

He popped it, and the Echoes crowded around. Their sound pulses intensified as they bombarded the engine compartment, building 3-D imagery in their minds from the reflected probes.

One of them recoiled, arms folded inward for self-defense. [Toxicity.]

[There is no danger,] one of the herders said. [Focus your intensity. The levels will not cause harm with brief exposure.]

The worried Echo ramped up its pulses, then relaxed its arms, satisfied.

[What does this conveyance use for propulsion?] the herder asked Sam.

"Gasoline, processed from oil—petroleum." The keys were already in the ignition. Sam cranked it. The engine rumbled to life.

"Okay, guys, stand back." He closed the door and wound the windows down, waiting for everyone to move back to the sidewalk, then he drove the car down the street. After a quick show of the acceleration and braking capabilities, he parked it on the opposite side of the street.

[It doesn't even fly,] one of the four corner Echoes pulsed in short, irritable sound bursts.

[This is a primitive society.] The herder's tone was meant to chastise. [Continue recording the lesson.]

Sam ignored the interplay. It wasn't his place to comment. "Maybe someday you'll be old enough to drive. I learned when I was sixteen years old."

[Years are your measurement of time,] the herder said.

"That's how we know how long things last." Sam waved. A flurry of sound pulses charted his movements. "Let's go."

The group followed him to a set of storefronts, filled with all manner of artifacts—men's and women's clothing, cooking utensils, and electronic devices. There was even a book store.

"You can buy most anything you need here," Sam said. "If I need a new soup spoon, they've got it."

Pulses erupted as the Vock tried to translate "soup" into Echo-speak. [Eating liquid?] The littlest one scoffed. [That isn't true.]

[There is research to show humans do consume liquid for a meal,] the herder explained.

[Why don't they just ingest the juices, like from a tarantur?] The littlest one made a quick, slurping noise that made Sam's skin crawl.

[Theirs was a vastly different culture from ours.]

Sam gestured to the other stores. "Here's where I bought my tablet. It's great for watching movies, or video chatting with friends, or sending them messages."

The youngest ones were prodding each other with discrete pulses, but most of the groups' attention stayed focused on Sam. The Vock kept a count of their inquiries. He'd need those, if the supervisor was going to let him keep the job beyond the end of the day.

"This book store is where I like to do my work." Sam pressed a hand to the glass. "I'll set up my laptop computer and write articles. A lot of what I create is information about life in the city, its habits and its people, places others would like to visit."

[You are a historian,] the second herder said.

"In a way, yes. My blog keeps track of life."

[Are the contents of this… blog still retrievable?]

Sam had to step outside his persona to answer this one. Hopefully the supervisor wouldn't mind. "A lot of electronic records were disrupted or destroyed." It made Sam's nausea worse to consider it. "Keep in mind, this is what my home planet was like a long, long time ago."

The littlest one peered in the window of the bookstore. [Are those blogs?]

"No. Those are books. We read them, using only our eyes and our hands."

[Like you do with your electronics?]

"Yes."

The littlest let out a blast of static. [It'd be easier to absorb all the information at once, then sort out what you need later.]

[Easier for us,] another little one said.

Lots of static.

[Learners, recall that human physiology is far different than ours, and their technology is stunted,] a herder said firmly. [They are adapting to our ways. It will take time.]

[They should just go back,] the littlest muttered.

Sam rapped his fingers on the bookstore window. The books twitched, their holographic images disrupted.

He knelt in front of the littlest Echo. "We can't."

#

The group was mostly silent for the rest of the tour. Sam showed them how to work a can opener, explored the limits of digital cameras—which was mostly lost on them, as they could barely interpret the recorded imagery—and explained how his clothing was made. It required a few excruciating minutes of the entire brood pawing at his shirt and jeans while sound pulses barraged him.

But it confirmed his suspicions.

When the walkthrough ended, none of them thanked Sam. Echoes didn't thank anyone. A job was a job and when it was done, there was either criticism or silence.

Sam took silence to be a good thing, but the idea of his and Laura's existence hinging on how their supervising species perceived their usefulness rankled him.

The supervisor was a dark-gray skinned creature, called a contributor, as tall as a herder but much bigger around. He had no name—the Echoes' sound signatures for each other didn't translate—which left Sam to dub him Mark, because he reminded Sam of a burly Latino at his last job in Sanitation & Maintenance.

[The brood you took demonstrated a retention and attentiveness score in the upper 90s,] Mark said. [This is above average for our interactive displays.]

Sam whistled. "Glad to hear it."

[They gave you no criticism.]

"They saw what life was like on a world that no longer exists."

[I have pulsed data regarding Earth. It remains in its orbit.]

"But life there isn't the same. It's—conquered. Ruined."

Mark's pulses intensify. [Your species brought punishment on itself, as did the others resettled here. It is our responsibility to reward those who do well and remove those who do not. Poor performance leads to re-education.]

He didn't signal the words, but Sam knew he meant Block Zero. Re-programming was a better term. Sam had to avoid this at all costs. Too many job failures, and he would have every last vestige of humanity scrubbed from his mind. "Of course. I am grateful my work performance pleased the visitors."

The Vock missed whatever Mark echoed, before providing the next translation. [Based on this, I recommend to the advisors that you be allowed to continue this job for the next six orbits. If this is not to your satisfaction, I will pass you along to the next department in need of refugee labor.]

"I accept your recommendation." Sam restrained the victory whoop he wanted to let off, because the Echo might see that as a challenge to his authority. But six orbits! It was nearly three years. It put Block Zero a long way out of the realm of possibility

[Your ration has been increased 10 percent accordingly. Continue above average scores and it shall rise another 10 percent in two orbits.]

"Thanks, Mark. I'll be ready for the next tour."

They both looked out over the dead street of the reconstructed Philadelphia. Mark manipulated a device on his torso, and the blue, cloudless sky vanished, revealing the familiar hazy green. Beyond the replica, Sam could see twenty more recreated neighborhoods from various Earth locales, stretching up the habitat's curved wall, and beyond that, hundreds from other worlds.

[Your planet was a fascinating place,] Mark said.

Sam wished he had some other job, one that didn't require him to revisit the past glory of his homeworld. Yet, one thought stayed with him as he finished twelve more tours, cleaned up the artifacts, and then rode the transport back to the platforms. It dogged his every step back along the walkways to the sprawling stacks of refugee housing protruding from the great curved shell of the habitat.

The Echoes used their pulses to pinpoint objects, but items lacking an electrical current—Sam's clothing, his bag, even the can opener—were indistinct.

The same gurnx bumped him and repeated its warning for him to stay in his place.

Sam knew his place wasn't here. It was on Earth—whatever was left of it.

But now that he knew of a weakness…

Humans were never meant to live this way. The time had come to prove it.

The End

Steve Rzasa

Steve Rzasa is the author of several novels of science-fiction, steampunk, and fantasy—with a bunch more in progress. He was first published in 2009 by Marcher Lord Press (now Enclave Publishing). His third novel, Broken Sight, received the 2012 Award for Speculative Fiction from the American Christian Fiction Writers. The Word Endangered (2016) and Man Behind the Wheel (2017) have both been nominated for the Realm Award in recent years. Steve grew up in Atco, New Jersey, and started writing stories in grade school. He received his bachelor's degree in journalism from Boston University, and worked for eight years at newspapers in Maine and Wyoming. He's been a librarian since 2008, most recently earning his Library Support Staff Certification from the American Library Association. He is the technical services librarian in Buffalo, Wyoming, where he lives with his wife and two boys. Steve's a fan of all things science-fiction and superhero and is also a student of history.

Email: steverzasa@gmail.com
Website: www.steverzasa.com

Her Majesty's Guardian

Donald S. Crankshaw

"It's eccentric," Alric said, "but surely it's not dangerous."

"The Council's vote was unanimous," Duke Richard said. He looked ridiculous in a bright yellow doublet. The color would make anyone look foolish, as the other old men seated around the table proved, but its gaiety was especially jarring against Richard's habitual dark expression. "You know your duty, Guardian."

Alric, in his customary black, stood out like a crow among canaries. He wanted to protest further, but he had no arguments left after the last hour's debate. More arguing would only convince them to give his task to someone else, and he couldn't do that to her. He felt a heavy weight settle on his chest as he bowed to the Duke. "I will do as you command, Your Grace. But I will never forgive myself." *Nor you.*

The Duke's expression softened. "No Guardian is glad of this duty, but it is what you must do to defend Ildor."

Ildor. Blessed home. The most powerful of the known kingdoms, rich in both gold and magic. And in generosity. What other country would take in the son of a murderer and raise him to a position of honor? In Eloun or Maltir, Alric would have been abandoned to survive on his own, if not sold as a slave. It was the royal dynasty, born of the most puissant bloodlines, which made Ildor what it was. They were not just the country's power and defense, but its very soul. Alas, no mortal soul was without stain.

Alric bowed once again but turned to go without answering the Duke. He had to stop once he entered the corridor to let his eyes adjust to the brightness. The sunlight through the eastern window illuminated the hallway with painful intensity, as every scrap of cloth, from carpet, to tapestry, to servant uniform, was an effulgent yellow. Tiana's work, of course. She loved yellow. He remembered how pleased she'd been with the yellow ribbon he'd given her when she was a child. She had worn it every day until it was frayed and faded.

Tiana still kept it, though she'd be embarrassed if she learned that he knew.

The servants watched him with wary eyes, wondering if the order had come. Fear, grief, relief, happiness, even guilt showed in their faces, in a hundred different combinations. Alric neither avoided nor sought their eyes. He had no desire for them to see confirmation in his. Only when he could find a quiet corner did he allow himself to weep, hand pressed against the locket hidden beneath his shirt. It pulsed like a tiny heartbeat with the life it contained.

#

Tiana's rooms were flanked by two Palace Guards in uniforms as yellow as everyone else's. One stepped forward as Alric approached, saying, "Guardian, Her Majesty left orders not to be disturbed."

Alric just looked at him, and the guard hastened to step back. By law and by magic, no one could impede the Guardian, not even the queen herself. Alric opened the door and entered Tiana's sitting room.

The queen stood on the balcony outside the open door. Alric crossed the carpet—also yellow, as was the upholstery of the chairs—to join her. The cool spring air was a welcome relief from the stifling heat radiating from the sitting room's hearth fire. Tiana turned and smiled at the sight of him.

"Alric!" she said. Her dress was yellow, but it had always been that color, and now so was her hair, which had been its usual brown yesterday. Looking closely, Alric saw that even her eyes had turned golden. Her smile faded. "No fair. You're still wearing black."

Tiana was a head shorter than he, but at fifteen, she was not yet fully grown. Alric had been her Guardian since before she was born. "You know that I'm immune to your magic," he told her. "All Guardians are."

"But not even your clothes changed."

"My possessions are as immune as I am."

"Really? What about the clothes you weren't wearing?"

"Nothing in my chambers was affected," he replied. "I was quite startled when I left them, however."

She giggled. "I can imagine. So tell me, what does everyone think of the new color?"

"I'm afraid that not everyone likes yellow as much as you do."

"I could make them like it," she said.

Alric felt a small chill at her casual tone. He had no doubt that she had the ability, but he wouldn't have believed that she was callous enough to bend people's wills. Not before today. "Why would you want to do that?"

"Oh, I suppose I shouldn't bother. Doesn't anyone else in the kingdom have good taste?"

"Even those who are fond of yellow aren't sure about quite so much of it. Tell me, why did you change the colors?"

"I like yellow."

"Was that the only reason?" he asked, not sure whether to be relieved at the innocuous answer. It didn't change his duty either way.

"I can't trust blue," she said, leaning close. "It hides death beneath still water. And red is always so forceful, so demanding. Green is standoffish. I'm not good enough for her, and I'm the queen! Yellow is the only color I can stand."

Alric sighed. Even as a child she had given personality to colors and shapes. He had thought she'd outgrown it, but now it had combined with a disturbing paranoia. Her father had shown a similar mistrust near the end. Mere jealousy for Tiana's affection could not explain his rages against Alric. The Council had been right. He crossed to the hearth, pulling the locket from the neck of his shirt.

"You've had that as long as I can remember," Tiana said, "but you've never shown me what's inside."

"No, I haven't," he said. "Did I ever tell you about my parents?"

"No. Is that what's in there? Portraits of your parents?"

"And something else, yes," he replied. "You should know that my mother was a murderer."

"Your *mother*?" she said. "I had always heard that you were the son of a murderer. I thought they meant your father."

"My father is the one she killed."

"Why would she do such a thing?"

"For me," Alric said. "My father and I fought often, and his beatings got worse as I grew older. He probably would have killed me eventually." He turned to face her, the locket still in his hand. "My mother loved my father, but she poisoned him to protect me."

"That's awful," she said. "But you say that like it's your fault. It's not."

"Isn't it? Blood tells, as much for me as for you." The locket opened as his fingers found the catch. His parents stared up at him: his father accusingly, his mother looking resigned. "I'm sorry, Your Majesty."

Alric drew a lock of fine white hair out of the locket and held it in the flame. He ignored the pain as the fire eagerly consumed the lock of hair.

"What are you doing?" Tiana cried. "You'll hurt your—" Her words choked off as she crumpled to the floor.

Ignoring his burned fingers, he knelt beside his queen and gathered her in his arms. She stared up at him, her eyes wide and mouth gasping. "What's happening to me?" she whispered. She wore the same terrified expression as when he had rescued her from an assassin three years ago.

"You're dying, Tiana," he told her gently. "Love demanded a terrible choice of me, just as it did my mother."

Her eyes went to the fire. He nodded, "A lock of your hair, taken when you were an infant." He remembered holding the baby girl in his arms as the alchemist cut the lock free. The circle of chanting priests had caused the nursery to ring with power. "Powerful spells bound you to it. It's what made me immune to your magic, and now that it's gone, you're dying."

"But you were my Guardian," she breathed.

"Ah, my queen. I was never guarding you. I was guarding Ildor *from* you." He smoothed the hair from her face and smiled sadly. "Like me, you are true to your blood. Everyone in the royal family goes mad eventually; tyranny and terror always follow. That is why there are Guardians." He kissed her brow and closed her staring eyes. "I love you, Tiana. But I love Ildor more."

The End

Donald S. Crankshaw has a Ph.D. in Electrical Engineering from MIT, which was more useful for writing fantasy than he had expected, though less helpful for writing science fiction than he had hoped. He has previously published stories in *Nature Futures*, *Daily Science Fiction*, and *Black Gate*. Donald lives in Boston with his wife and fellow writer, Kristin Janz. Together, they edit and publish *Mysterion*, a webzine of Christian-themed speculative fiction at www.mysteriononline.com.

Dragon Moon

Linda Burklin

"I don't get many requests to do soles," the tattoo artist said.

Darla clenched her teeth. "No kidding."

She had slathered her foot with a topical anesthetic, but the effects were wearing off, and she was starting to wonder how she was going to walk home.

"You walked here, didn't you?" Greg, the tattoo guy, must have read her mind. "Why don't I get my wife to take you home? I don't know how far away you live, but it's going to seem a lot farther going back."

"It's just a few blocks from here," Darla said, "but I have to admit a ride would be nice."

When Greg's wife Lacy dropped her off, Darla hopped to the stairs leading to her little apartment over the garage. After trying various options, she got up the stairs by sitting down and pushing herself up one step at a time using her arms and her "good" foot. She hoped Mom wasn't watching her through the kitchen window—and she was glad the weather had warmed up enough to keep her backside from freezing as she inched up the stairs.

After crawling through the door, she flopped onto her couch. She had expected the tattoo to hurt, but she hadn't been prepared for the reality of the pain on the sole of her foot. Still, it'd be worth it if it made David smile. She pulled her foot up and looked at the bottom. It was hard to tell what it was going to look like when the swelling went down.

Two days later, she had her answer. Though the foot still hurt, the design was clear. Small blue overlapping scales covered the bottom of her foot. Lighter in the middle and darker around the edges, hints of green and purple glinted in the darker borders of the scales, but the overall color was blue. After putting on her socks and clogs, she hobbled over to the main house and into the kitchen.

"Where have you been all weekend?" Mom asked. "David's been asking about you."

"I, uh, have something special to show David, and it wasn't ready till now."

"Oh? What is it?"

"It's something private. Between him and me."

Mom's tolerant smile changed to a look of alarm as Darla limped past.

"What happened to your foot? You're limping!"

"I hurt it a little, but it's already getting better. I promise." She couldn't risk Mom being concerned enough to look at the foot.

Without pausing, she continued on toward the den that had been converted into a hospital room for her little brother David.

"Darla!" His face lit up when she walked in the door. "I missed you!"

"I missed you too, buddy." She sat down on the end of his bed.

"Remember that dream you told me about last week?"

His brow wrinkled in thought. His bald head made his skin seem even more fragile and transparent than it had before. "The dragon dream?"

"Yes, that's the one. Can you tell it to me again?"

"Well, I dreamed I saw a huge blue dragon flying in the sky. He was so beautiful! And somehow, in my dream, I knew he was going somewhere wonderful. Just looking at him filled me up with joy. But when I called and begged him to let me ride on his back and fly with him, he just said 'I'm not there yet.' Do you think there are blue dragons in heaven and that they'd let me ride them?"

Darla smiled at him. "I dunno, David. But I know if heaven has blue dragons, you can ride them as much as you want. Look, I want to show you something."

She took the sock off her right foot and swung it up on to the bed so David could see it. His eyes widened till she feared they would pop, and his thin face lit up with a hundred-watt smile.

"You got a dragon-scale tattoo? That is so awesome! What did Mom say?"

"Mom doesn't know. It's our secret, okay?"

He nodded, grinning. "Are you going to get the other foot done?"

She had expected this question, had been bracing for it.

"Yes, as soon as this one stops hurting and itching, I'll get the other one done. We can pretend I am a blue dragon—in disguise. It'll be our secret."

By June, two months later, scales covered Darla's legs up to her knees. Her car savings fund took a hit, but she didn't really care because her scaly feet made David happy. She began working extra odd jobs to cover the cost of her ink. She still hadn't told her parents. She wore sneakers and jeans most of the time so they had no reason to suspect that under those faded jeans, her legs were covered with scales.

David was thrilled. "If you have dragon feet, you should have a dragon name. A girl dragon name."

They spent several delightful days discussing and discarding every dragonish name they could think of, before settling on the name "Indiglory," to emphasize the beautiful color of the scales and the general gloriousness of being a dragon. From that moment on, David never called her Darla again unless Mom or Dad was in earshot.

That evening, however, Mom climbed up to Darla's apartment after David had fallen asleep.

"Darla, you know I'm thrilled you and David have such a close bond. I would never have believed a nineteen-year-old and a nine-year-old would be such good pals. But Dad and I are worried about you."

"Why? Because I care about my little brother?"

"No, dear—because you care too much. When was the last time you went to a movie with your friends? How long has it been since you talked about taking college classes? What kind of life are you going to have left after David dies?"

"Don't say that! Why do you give up so easily? He's not gonna die! He's getting all the right medicine! I'm helping him get better!"

"I don't deny that you're helping him *feel* better, Darla. But you know as well as I do that the chances are very slim he'll recover."

Darla put her hands over her ears. "Don't *say* that!"

#

The next Saturday she kept another appointment with Greg, wearing a long skirt that reached to her ankles.

"I'm ready for the thighs now," she said, trembling inside.

She was a modest girl who hated baring her thighs to anyone. But Lacy had been working side-by-side with Greg on her tattoos, and that somehow made it more bearable.

The scales had been gradually increasing in size as they crept higher up her legs. She would never have believed she would think her legs looked beautiful covered with scales, but she did. It helped that Greg and Lacy were such gifted artists. Getting the inside of her thighs done was even more excruciating than her feet, but at least she didn't have to walk on them. She lay with tears streaming down her cheeks, but she didn't move or cry out. If David could tolerate what he'd been through, who was she to complain about the temporary pain of a tattoo?

She knew that somehow, her tattoos kept David going. Each new addition to her scales delighted him. They spent hours speculating on the details of dragon life. Since the first tattoo, she had read him two whole series of books about dragons, making a point to choose books that portrayed them in a positive, heroic light. They now referred to his room as his "lair," and they piled all his most prized possessions under his hospital-style bed to stand in as his treasure hoard.

That night, as she lay awake in bed with her thighs burning, she asked herself how far she was willing to go. She had once thought she would stop at the soles of her feet. Now, she often thought of herself as Indiglory rather than Darla. How would she feel about her beautiful dragon legs twenty years from now? Thirty? It didn't matter. David mattered. He never talked about his illness anymore. The dragon dream had captured his imagination—and for the rest of her life, the tattoos would remind her of her brother.

By July her back had been inked, complete with folded-up wings and tattooed spikes down the middle—except for the part where a rider might sit. Her car savings were severely depleted. But when she put a swimsuit on under her clothes, and then showed her back to David, he gasped in delight.

"Oh, Indiglory, the spikes are perfect! I always imagined them a solid indigo blue!"

At that moment, Mom walked into the room and stopped dead in her tracks, her hand over her mouth. Darla stood there in her swimsuit, her blue-scaled legs bare.

"Please tell me you just drew on yourself with markers," said Mom.

"Isn't it awesome?" David said. "She's my dragon sister now! Her new name is Indiglory."

"Turn around," Mom ordered. Her voice shook in a way that Darla had never heard before.

Darla turned around, exposing her back to her mother's scrutiny. She heard the horrified gasp, but she kept a smile on her face and winked at David.

"I have nothing to say," Mom said. "I'm speechless. I'll let your father deal with this."

She all but ran from the room and slammed the door, but Darla could still hear the sobs that echoed from the hallway.

She braced herself for the confrontation to come, wishing she could keep her parents *and*

David happy. It would have been easier to take if Dad had been angry rather than sorrowful.

"I can't order you to stop defacing your body," he said, "because you're an adult and you're earning the money to do this to yourself. But I just want you to know it grieves me to think you didn't believe your body was attractive by itself. You'll always be beautiful to me, Darla, but the tattoos don't make you any *more* beautiful than you were before."

"It's not about beauty or vanity, Dad. It's about David. It's a private world he and I share. A world where I'm a dragon called Indiglory and he's my little friend."

"He *has* been talking about dragons a lot lately," said Mom. "He barely notices his physical discomforts because he's so focused on his fantasy. I can't fault you on your motives, Darla."

#

Now that the cat was out of the bag, so to speak, Darla could get her hands and arms done. Lacy had misgivings about doing her hands.

"You may regret it someday," she said. "I know you're doing it for your brother, but someday you're going to want to have your own life. It might be hard for you to do some things if you look like a giant blue lizard."

Darla said nothing. Greg and Lacy were a second family to her now. How could they question her when she was single-handedly keeping David alive? Back in the winter, the doctor had said David would be gone before Easter—yet here it was August and he could still go outside every afternoon, to talk and eat and smile and laugh. Whatever the future cost might be, it was worth it. Her hands were inked with beautiful little scales, none larger than a quarter of an inch across. That night, Mom cried at the supper table.

Eyebrows were raised at work when Darla showed up with her newly inked hands and arms, but since it didn't affect her ability to stock the shelves at Wal-Mart, she didn't suffer any repercussions.

By the beginning of October, her neck and chest were done.

"Don't even think about asking us to do your face," Greg said. "I promise you'll regret it. Maybe not right away, but years from now when you have children of your own."

"Chill," she said. "I'm not ready to get my face done either."

#

Temperatures fell as autumn progressed. During the warmest part of the day, Darla wheeled David outside to the back yard, after all but burying him under blankets and putting a thick fuzzy hat on his head. They talked about their private world and watched the leaves blow off the trees one by one.

"You're almost all dragon now, Indiglory," David said. "But you're still my sister, too. I like having a dragon for a sister. It makes me fearless."

Darla smiled. "You've always been fearless, David. I'm the coward."

He was even thinner now, and fear clutched at her heart when she looked at him. She couldn't still pretend he was getting better, or deny what her eyes saw every day: her little brother was fading away.

When the shorter days of November came, they had to give up going outside. Darla kept David busy helping her draw a map of Indiglory's home world. For hours at a time, they discussed the history behind each feature on the map. David's thin face lit up each time she laid the map out on the floor so she could work on it while he watched and made suggestions.

On December 3rd, the first snow fell, blanketing everything in white powder and transforming their little neighborhood into an enchanted dream world.

"Can't you stay with me tonight?" David asked. "On a snowy night like this, I could use a dragon to keep me warm."

How could she say no? She ran to her apartment to get an old pair of shorts and a t-shirt to sleep in. She giggled to think of having a sleepover with her little brother.

"Won't you be cold with shorts on, Indiglory?"

"Dragons don't get cold," she said. "We keep our favorite humans warm."

She climbed into the bed beside him, on the side without the tubes and wires, and carefully folded her arms around his impossibly fragile body as he snuggled next to her.

Mom came in. "What's going on here?"

"We're having a sleepover," David said. "My dragon sister is keeping me warm."

"Mom, could you please open the curtains before you turn off the light?" Darla asked. "We want the moonlight to shine in on us tonight."

David yawned. "The first full moon after the first snow is the dragon moon."

A frisson of excitement trilled down Darla's spine. *The dragon moon.* It sounded so mysterious and tantalizing.

They lay awake for some time, whispering together and watching the moonlight on the snow. Finally, David fell asleep and Darla felt her own eyes drooping.

When she awoke, the moon rode high in the sky and she felt something was wrong—not with David, but with herself. Ever so gently, she withdrew her arms from around David and slid from the high hospital bed onto the floor. Her feet felt weird. She walked over to where the moonlight came in through the window and looked down. They weren't *her* feet anymore. They were beautiful reptilian feet, covered with glittering scales and complete with dangerous-looking talons.

She held her hands out. They, too, had transformed into gleaming claws. The muscles of her arms and legs rippled under real dragon scales. She could hardly believe it. Turning to gaze down at David, she was puzzled at how far away he looked, until she realized dragons were taller than girls. She flexed her shoulders and felt her wings unfurling behind her as they filled with the blood pumped from her dragon heart. If she didn't get out of the house soon, she wouldn't fit through the door.

Leaning down, she scooped up David in her scaly arms. He opened his eyes and they widened in the moonlight. His face filled with joy.

"It's the dragon moon!" he said. "It made you real, Indiglory!"

"I have to get outside before I get too big. Do you want to come with me?"

He nodded, his eyes huge and bright in his pinched little face. He disconnected himself from all the tubes and wires and pulled on his old red bathrobe, now ridiculously big for him.

Hugging him to her scale-covered chest, she tiptoed through the house to the family room door, her long spiked tail dragging behind her. David giggled as she squeezed through the sliding door and popped out onto the patio.

"Come on," she said. "Time to climb on my back. What could be better than riding a dragon on the night of the dragon moon? The snow can't make you cold if you're with me."

She bent down and kissed his forehead with her new lips before he climbed onto her back and hooked his skinny little legs around her shoulders. Dropping to all fours, she spread her enormous wings out till they reached from side to side of their big backyard. Seething hot blood coursed through her veins and filled her fierce dragon heart with strength and courage.

"Hang on tight!" she said.

David wrapped his little arms around her newly-lengthened neck. Even though she had never had wings before, she knew how to use them. Her mighty muscles lifted the wings and then brought them down. Just like that, her feet left the ground. A few swift strokes and she and David soared skyward above the glittering moonlit world.

"Where are we going?" David asked, his voice full of joy.

"Wherever we want!" she answered, and they both laughed.

#

Denise Emerson lay awake in bed, worrying about David, her beloved only son. He was so frail now—he could slip away at any time. Thank goodness Darla was with him. If anything happened, Darla would let her know.

She heard a sound she couldn't place at first. It sounded like someone dragging something heavy through the house while making clicking noises. Yikes!

She nudged her husband. "Mark! I think there's someone in the house."

He sat up, alert. They heard the sliding glass door in the family room open.

"You stay here," He swung his feet over the side of the bed and stuffed his feet into his slippers.

"No, I'm coming with you." The icy fingers of fear gripped her heart, and she didn't want to be alone.

Mark grabbed a baseball bat from the hall closet and they crept into the family room, where the sliding door stood wide open. Hand in hand, they ran to the door in time to see an enormous blue dragon spreading out its wings in the moonlight. David sat on the beast's back in his old red bathrobe. His arms were wrapped around its scaly neck, and while they watched, he laid his head down against that mighty neck. The dragon beat its huge wings, rose gracefully into the air, and soared across the full moon in the cold night sky.

She should be screaming or calling out, but instead she just watched that dragon—it must be Darla, somehow—fly away with her son. Hot tears welled from her eyes and cooled instantly on her cold cheeks.

"Well, they're gone," Mark said. "Both of our babies." He sounded as forlorn as she felt.

He pulled the sliding door closed behind them when they finally walked back inside, and she said, "Don't lock it. In case they come back."

"They're not coming back."

He led her back to David's room, the room where he had fought for life for over a year now. Eight months of that time had been a gift—a gift from the dragon that had once been their daughter. The door of David's room stood open and she heard Mark gasp in surprise as he crossed the threshold. She pushed past him to look, and then held her breath.

Both of their children still lay curled up on the bed. Darla's eyes were open, and wet with tears. Her pearly white arms wrapped around the lifeless body of her little brother. There was no sign of a tattoo.

"Your tattoos!" Mark said. "What happened to your tattoos?"

Darla sat up and stared at her arms in the moonlight. "They're gone!" Her voice quivered with both grief and puzzlement.

Denise nodded, tears springing to her eyes as the answer came to her. "They belonged to Indiglory. I guess she took them when she took David."

Darla looked at David's body, lovingly stroked the soft bald head one last time.

"David's dream came true, Mom. He rode home on a dragon."

The End

Linda Burklin

Linda has been a storyteller and writer since childhood. Raised primarily in Africa, she wrote for and edited her college newspaper for two years while earning her English degree. For seventeen years, she has taught writing classes to her own and other homeschooled children and authored the Story Quest creative writing curriculum. She has written a memoir, several short stories, and five novels. Her passion is speculative fiction.

Find out more about Linda at: http://www.lindaburklin.com

The Other Edge

C.W. Briar

Astronaut Varik Babel reached out to keep from rotating in front of the video display. He drifted backwards until his feet touched lightly against the wall, and he glanced out the spaceship window. His brief look stretched into a lingering gaze. They were orbiting over the ultramarine waters of the Mediterranean and the tan coasts of Europe and Africa.

"… Would you agree, commander?" asked the reporter on the communications display.

Oh, cripes! What was the question?

Like a student called on by his teacher while daydreaming, he flipped back a page in his memory, trying to recall what had been asked. What could he say to redirect the interviewer? He must look like a fool.

Janice Widowicz, the five-person crew's biology specialist and youngest member, rescued him. "We can't see it from this part of the ship right now," she said, minimizing her French-Canadian accent. "But we do have a magnificent view of Earth. *Ciao* to everyone watching from Italy."

"Have you seen *Angel One* yet?" the reporter asked.

"Yes," Janice said. "We're orbiting alongside it at a distance of approximately six hundred meters."

Varik smoldered with frustration. *Hadn't the reporter been listening when the last five interviewers asked the same thing? We are six hundred meters from the greatest discovery in history. Stop wasting our time.*

It had taken humanity almost a decade of work to reach this moment. When scientists began broadcasting laser communications to probes around Mars, they didn't expect to hear replies from the asteroid belt beyond the Red Planet. An unidentified object was broadcasting a signal that counted up and down in increments of ten, and every nation denied it belonged to them.

The first known alien artifact, a spacecraft, had been found. NASA named it *Angel One* and declared its plan to bring the object to earth's orbit.

Varik remembered the announcement well. He had been a pilot for the Air Force at the time, but within a week of hearing the news, he submitted his résumé to NASA. This was going to be a monumental event. He needed to be a part of it, even if only in some small way. By hard work and luck, he earned more than a small role. He was chosen as commander of *Unity*, the space shuttle built to intercept and investigate *Angel One*.

But being on the first crew sent to explore an alien spacecraft meant enduring the media day after day. Varik knew what the next question would be before the interviewer said it.

"Can you describe the alien ship for us?"

The *Unity* crew members looked at one another. Lance Ishikawa, the engineering specialist, took the question.

"The vessel is approximately two hundred meters long, making it three times longer than our ship and four times longer than the old space shuttles. It's shaped like a swan with a long neck, except the wings are short and the body is round like a disc. The box structures on the wings are possibly thrusters."

"What color is it?"

"The spacecraft's skin is extraordinary," Janice said, her accent more prominent with her excited tone. "It's not a single color, especially when sunlight reflects off of it. The best description for it is slightly darkened mother-of-pearl."

The interviewer directed a few questions to the rest of the crew, British pilot Callum Mills and German mission specialist Emma Stadt. He then said "Commander Babel" and paused for a response. He probably wanted to confirm Varik was paying attention this time.

"Yes?" Varik said.

"Are you and the rest of your team proud to have won the Second Space Race?"

Varik nearly scoffed at the question. "This mission has never been about nationalistic one-upmanship, and I have a lot of respect for the Russian cosmonauts and the Chinese. I've worked with both."

He sighed. The reporter was sidetracking him. "The priority of our mission has always been to explore this artifact left by our unknown intergalactic neighbors. This moment is for all of humanity. Our ship is called *Unity*, after all."

"And there certainly will be a large percentage of humanity watching," the reporter said. "Experts predict your mission will be the biggest televised event in history. How does it feel to be watched by billions of people?"

It feels like you're wasting everyone's time with idiotic commentary, that's what.

Janice patted Varik on the shoulder. She had witnessed enough of his rants to know how he truly felt.

Varik forced an ambassadorial smile. "I would like to tell those billions of people to stay tuned. The course of human history will change forever after today."

After a few more exchanges with the crew, the reporter signed off with an awkward catch phrase that was, based on his grin, nowhere near as clever as he thought it was. After a cut to black, the comm's display changed to a live feed of Nick Costa. The balding man was the capsule communicator, which meant he bore the famous "Houston" call sign and served as the voice of the command center.

"That's it, folks," he said. "It's just us now. Are you ready to make history?"

The crew let out a collective sigh.

"It's about time," Callum said.

"Sorry, *Unity*. Everyone down here is just as eager as you, trust me." Nick checked his watch. "We're only a little behind schedule. Varik, Janice, and Ishikawa, suit up for the walk."

The distractions stopping them from the mission had passed. Emma drifted toward the flight deck with Callum, laughing at a comment he had whispered. Janice and Ishikawa leapt off the wall and propelled themselves like torpedoes toward the airlock. An hour and multiple interviews ago, Varik would have gladly joined them. Instead, he lingered in front of the comms display, fuming. He could see Nick speaking with someone off camera.

"Nick?" He used his friend's name rather than his call sign to indicate what he had to say was personal.

Nick turned to him and inserted his earpiece. "Yeah, Varik?"

He scowled. "Seriously, what was that bullcrap? Nine interviews? We're astronauts, not TV hosts."

"Calm down. That's part of being a hero. Plus, we need to pay the bills. Interviews excite the taxpayers, and excited taxpayers don't complain about funding NASA."

"There's a six-hundred-foot alien vessel orbiting Earth. Keep that on camera and they'll fund us for the next century."

Nick tipped a lopsided grimace at him, letting Varik know he didn't want to have this conversation. "The politicians push for this stuff. I know you hate politics, but they're the ones who ultimately pay us, so just deal with it."

"Sorry, how could I forget?" Varik apologized sarcastically. "It's not enough to explore the most significant find of all time. It's all about winning the race for ol' red, white, and blue. We gotta scratch Uncle Sam's beard, right?"

Nick shot glances over his shoulders. "Watch what you're saying."

"I am. I toned down what I wanted to say."

"No, I mean the president has his CIA bulldogs here around the clock. They've got their noses so deep in NASA's business, I can't fart without them knowing it."

He checked over his shoulders again. "It's not been announced publicly yet, but Russia moved up their launch date by ten days. You have two weeks before they join you, and I agree with Washington and London that we need to get all potentially lethal tech out of *Angel One* before Kashnikov can get his hands on it."

Kashnikov was Russia's president and a throwback to the unpredictable, militaristic leaders of decades past.

"This is why I prefer science," Varik said. "It's so much purer and simpler than politics."

"Reality is messier than a laboratory." Nick shooed him with his fingers. "Go get your suit on. I'm dying to see what's on that ship."

So was Varik. At that reminder, his curiosity and excitement overwhelmed his frustrations. "You really know how to sweet-talk me."

Nick smiled. "Godspeed, Varik."

#

In the final moments before the spacewalk, all chatter on the radios went quiet. Everyone involved in the mission, both in orbit and on Earth, waited to see if the suits would respond correctly to the vacuum of space. Varik heard only the hiss of the depressurizing airlock and the beat of his pulse. The plastic smell of his spacesuit filled his nose.

"Pressurization is at zero," Varik said over the radio, breaking the silence. "My air is still good. Janice, what's your status?"

"I'm good," she responded from within her own suit. She tapped twice on her visor.

"Ishikawa?"

"No issues here."

"Excellent. Houston, we're ready."

Nick responded, "All right. Stay put, *Unity*." A few seconds later, presumably after affirming system readiness with the flight director, Nick announced, "Mission is go."

Those three words thrilled Varik just as much as the booster thrust had when they took off from Earth.

All three astronauts grabbed the bar over their heads, then Varik flipped the door's safety override and pressed the control button. The indicator light changed from yellow to red, and the door opened in a slow, silent yawn. Their target—the mottled, iridescent alien craft—loomed nearby. It was orbiting Earth with them at five hundred kilometers per minute.

Varik leaned out of the airlock. "I see *Angel One*."

He could also see *Aquila* clinging to the ship's back. NASA and the European Space Agency, ESA, had designed and launched *Aquila* within a mere twenty months of finding *Angel One*. The unmanned ship had operated as a rocket-powered claw machine that grabbed the interstellar prize and brought it back from the asteroid belt.

"Houston, are you receiving my helmet's camera feed?"

A delay, then, "Affirmative. We're watching with anticipation."

At long last, here we go.

He bounded out of *Unity* and soared over the wide, blue expanse of the Pacific. The artifact hung gleaming against the even wider expanse of black space. *Angel One* was aptly named. Its wings stood out at its sides, and sunlight reflected from its surface in an array of colors.

"She's beautiful," Varik said.

"Yes, she is," Nick replied through the spacesuit's speaker. "Slow your approach, lover boy."

Varik realized how quickly he was gliding toward the alien craft. His jump was on target, but unless he corrected his speed, his arrival at the alabaster hull would be a crash. He pressed his thumbs against his ring fingers, activating a short burst from his jetpack's reverse thrusters. His body cocked sideways, and his velocity slowed.

Angel One filled his visor. While en route, everything seemed familiar, giving him déjà vu from his hours in the simulator.

Then he touched the ship.

To his surprise, the hull deformed like gelatin under his fingers and toes. Waves rippled through the surface until, as if suddenly drawn tight, the material stiffened and reformed its original shape. The shuddering caused Varik to slip. He slid along the vessel, the difficulty of weightlessness vividly apparent as he tried to gain traction. Only by using his jetpack and catching his boot in a groove did he finally stop.

"Varik, are you okay?" Nick asked. In the back of his mind, Varik realized the question was being repeated. He had been too occupied to answer the first time.

"Affirmative, Houston. I'm fine."

"Your heart rate shot up, and you were cursing into the mic. What's going on?"

"Sorry, I just got surprised. The ship felt … rubbery or organic, like I tried to get traction on a whale carcass. It's rigid now, though."

A female voice came through the speaker. "This is Janice. Varik, am I clear to come over?"

Varik turned his back on *Angel One* and faced *Unity*. Janice and Ishikawa waved from the airlock doorway. "Yeah, Jan. Aim for me. It's easier to grab hold where the ship widens."

"Okay. Coming to you now."

Janice leapt out over the earth, followed a few seconds later by Ishikawa. From Varik's perspective, they looked like giants sliding over the surface of Asia. Wide, circular clouds, the telltale sign of a cyclone, churned off the shore of India. From orbit, even a violent storm looked beautiful and calm.

"Don't look down if you're afraid of heights," Varik said.

"Har, har," Ishikawa replied.

"Earth looks stunning from up here." He felt like they had the entire world to themselves. "Everything is serene. I could get used to this."

"Don't get too comfortable," Nick said. "I don't want you taking off your helmet and finding out how welcoming space really is."

"No worries, Houston."

"Okay. *Unity*, we're putting your audio on public broadcast now. Remember to switch to the private channel if there's anything you don't want Moscow or the general public to hear." After a pause, Nick said, "This is Houston. Commander Babel, care to share what it's like up there?"

Varik collapsed into his thoughts. The moment had come. He had long wondered how many months Neil Armstrong spent pondering his words for the lunar proclamation. The "one small step" line still reverberated almost a century later, and Varik's next words would be no less significant.

After clearing his throat and drawing in a long breath, he said, "If we, the people of Earth, are united by science, then nothing is impossible for us. The *Unity* crew has boarded *Angel One*." Varik waited for the applause in ground control to die down in his headset. "Widowicz and Ishikawa are almost to me. I see no doors or windows, an indication the spacecraft was possibly unmanned."

Varik knocked on the hull with his gloved knuckles. It felt hard but thin and hollow, like a pane of glass. "The exterior of *Angel One* is made from an unfamiliar material. It's mottled and glossy. Even more unusual is its rigidity. At first touch, it rippled significantly, but now it's as solid as titanium. Man, the folks in materials analysis are going to have a field day with this stuff."

"That could explain the unusual readings from *Aquila* when it docked with *Angel One*," Ishikawa said. He and Janice had almost reached the ship.

"You're right. I'm going to— Hold on! It's changing again."

The metallic structure began to dilate at the spot where Varik had knocked on it. The dimple gaped and widened to a round hole large enough for them to fit through. Varik stuck his head in the hole and shined his helmet lamp inside. He gulped air from his suit, unsure of how long he had been holding his breath.

"Houston, are you getting this?"

"We are. It's incredible."

The other two astronauts arrived, and they all crowded the opening. Their lights reflected off the white interior wall and silvery, grate-like floor and ceiling. Varik glanced down the throat of the ship, boring a tunnel through the darkness with his lamp.

"We seem to have activated an opening," Varik said. "We can see the interior of the ship's neck. It's not pressurized, nor do we see any signs of life yet, but it does look like it could have been manned at one time. Perhaps it still is."

Varik clambered forward, slowly, until his torso was inside the hole. He searched for movement. Something latched onto his spacesuit at the hip. Varik recoiled, flailing slowly and awkwardly in the zero gravity.

"I'm sorry," Janice said, laughter tinging her accent. "I didn't mean to startle you, Commander. I just wanted to remind you not to touch anything that looks biological. The last thing we need is to pass along a dangerous bacterium to Earth."

Varik let out a strong sigh. His breath reflected off his visor and tousled the front of his hair.

"Too bad," Ishikawa interjected. "I was hoping to keep the flesh-eating parasites as pets."

"*Unity*?" Nick said. "That reminds me. Did you bring the Taser?"

If Varik could have beaten his forehead against his faceplate, he would have. How many times had Nick regurgitated this topic? After broadcasting himself clearing his throat, Varik said, "Uh, no, Houston. I left it in the ship."

"You do realize you are potentially endangering yourself and your crew, correct? There may be hostile entities inside."

"So be it." Varik pulled the rest of his body into *Angel One*. "*Unity* questions the wisdom of carrying a weapon while making first contact with a more advanced species. I would rather risk my life than risk this moment."

"Suit yourself, but note NASA recommends you be prepared."

Ishikawa, the crew's resident fanatic of classic science fiction and horror, said, "Varik, keep your mouth closed when you meet 'em. You don't want them laying any babies in your chest."

The stationary helmet prevented Varik from casting a sideways glance at the specialist. "Ishikawa, I suspect Houston and Director Phillips are not keen on their astronauts recording frivolous banter at this crucial moment."

"Sorry, sir."

Nick snickered.

The grated floor and ceiling were segmented into a grid of diamond-shaped tiles. Varik glided over the checkerboard pattern like a chess piece, moving toward the nose and hopefully the cockpit of *Angel One*. His narrow light beam revealed an area where the walls curled in, choking off all but an open doorway in the ship's neck. He advanced through it, expecting to find computer terminals, seats, and other equipment in the forward room. Instead, he discovered … nothing.

To his disappointment, the room was as empty as a newly made coffin. The only other doorway doubled back down a second hallway that paralleled the first. He twisted his body to and fro, panning his light over the walls in hopes of finding more. How strange for such a prominent extension of the ship to be empty.

Janice, who had followed him into the room, must have sensed his confusion. She offered, "We can return later to swab for DNA and chemical samples."

"Commander?" Ishikawa called through the radio. "I think I've found something."

Varik moved to the doorway, then used a slight burst from his jetpack to fly down the hall to Ishikawa.

"I noticed one of the floor panels sticking up higher than the others." Ishikawa's wide, excited eyes were visible through his faceplate. "Can you help me with it? I think there's something underneath."

Ishikawa and Varik took crowbars out of the toolkits in their packs, then slid them under the corners of the panel. It guarded its secret well. Varik strained his back while prying the stubborn panel up enough to slide his fingers under the metal. Once the men had a decent grip, they widened their stances and lifted it together. Varik groaned through gritted teeth.

When the panel reached waist height, they let go and floated backwards. Janice swooped in and shined her light at the substructure they had revealed. Her voice rising, she exclaimed, "It's a container!"

"Janice, what's in it?" Nick asked with equal excitement.

Varik regained his orientation and glided to the raised compartment. Janice was holding one of the many clear, sludge-filled bags stowed beneath the panel, squeezing its contents. She announced, "It's green and fibrous but seems to be moist."

Mission Specialist Emma Stadt, watching the video feed from aboard *Unity*, spoke up for the first time since the spacewalk. "Is the matter organic?"

"I don't know." Janice pressed the end of the bag, thinning the contents in one corner. "It resembles algae. If … if it is …" She trailed off as she turned it over several times. "We might have found an alien organism."

Hairs rose on Varik's neck. He winked, activating the helmet's camera. The picture of the bag in Janice's hands displayed for a few seconds on the side of his visor, then disappeared. The sludge looked like a green version of the oatmeal they ate for breakfast, but he had never seen anything so magnificent.

Alien organic matter.

"Don't jump to conclusions," Janice warned. "It might be synthetic."

"Manufactured matter is still an incredible find," Nick said. "Will you be able to send some down to us in the drop pods?"

"We should be able to," Janice said. "I'll grab more bags."

"How much of that stuff do you think *Angel One* is hauling?" Ishikawa asked. "There's hundreds of floor panels in this hall, and they might all have bags like this under them."

"I don't know," Varik said. "Janice, grab a few and let's proceed. I want get as much exploration as possible out of our oxygen tanks."

Next they explored the halls that traversed the wide, circular body of the ship. The passages were bent into narrow, meandering arcs that never straightened for more than a few meters. Because of this, Varik's light carved out only a short distance of visibility. Shadows peeked around every curve, and the thought of being ambushed by aliens defending their ship became a genuine concern. The complete lack of environmental sounds and the inability to run away worsened his nerves.

Why did Ishikawa have to mention Alien? Varik would never confess it, but the movie, which had given him nightmares as a child, was feeding into his active and jittery imagination. He sensed movement at the edge of the darkness. Nothing materialized. He knew better than to expect lurking, acid-filled monsters, but someone built *Angel One*, and they might not be taking kindly to trespassing humans.

Get ahold of yourself. He's got you spooked over a movie that's as old as your father. You're supposed to be a man of science.

Nonetheless, his anxiety persisted. He felt as though he were diving in the shark-infested ruins of a sunken ship. Halls existed for a reason—so inhabitants could move about.

Were those inhabitants pursuing them as his intuition insisted, baring their teeth or weapons?

Varik slapped his helmet, trying to dislodge the unnerving thought. The artifact had been drifting in distant orbit for years, if not centuries or millennia. Not even basic life forms had ever been proven to survive under such conditions.

"Are you all right?" Janice asked.

"Yeah, I'm fine." Varik clutched wildly in his mind for an excuse. "I thought my speaker cut out, but I hear you loud and clear."

"This seems very inefficient," Ishikawa said.

"What does?"

"The halls. Why curve them? It complicates navigation."

"You're thinking like a *Homo sapiens*," Janice said. "Instead, translate the ship's design into clues about the travelers."

Varik found a room that branched off from the hall. "Something tells me our Janice is going to become a professor of xenosociology."

She chuckled. "Sounds like a good fallback plan to me."

Varik halted at the offset doorway and swept the next room with his light before entering. The chamber was kidney-shaped, and its white walls had a texture similar to tree bark. A bundle of green tubes hung from the ceiling and drifted lazily like seaweed in calm waters. Most intriguing was the array of stump-like fixtures that protruded from the floor.

"Houston," Varik said. "We have, uh … forty objects of unknown purpose in this room. They're brown, approximately fifty centimeters in height, and round with ridged edges."

"They look like giant peanut butter cups," Ishikawa added as he hovered over the top of one.

Varik pointed at his own lips with a jab, a gesture meant to remind Ishikawa their audio was being recorded for posterity. "Thank you, Ishikawa. I'm sure the people of Earth will be thrilled to know aliens travelled across the cosmos to bring us chocolate."

Each of the objects had a tall, curved plate that extended up from one side. When Varik pushed against the nearest one, it moved.

"The objects are fastened to the floor but do rotate. They have straps on these vertical portions."

"Chairs," Janice suggested. She turned to Varik, but the glare from his light veiled her face. "I'd bet my last oxygen tank they're chairs."

Varik nodded. He pressed the top of one seat. It compressed under his hand. "They're cushioned. I think Janice is right on this one. That makes forty passengers, at least. Where are they?"

Further searching revealed two similar rooms, tripling the number of seats. But they did not find any advanced life forms, living or dead. They also became disoriented by the roundabout courses of the halls, unsure if they were moving toward the ship's interior or exterior. Twice the labyrinthine corridors doubled back for no apparent reason.

Varik was considering how they might map the halls when Janice said, "Do you feel that?"

He spun to face the others, and his helmet scraped along the ceiling as he continued drifting. Janice was in the back of their group, enveloped up to her shoulders in darkness until

Varik aimed his light at her. She pressed both hands against the wall.

"The ship is vibrating."

Varik reached out, dragging his gloved fingers over the wall. He felt it too. Faintly. "The ship's active!" he blurted out, then grimaced for having shouted into the microphone. More calmly, he asked their pilot, "Callum, do you see anything out there? Maybe lights or movement?"

In his deep, bullfrog voice, Callum muttered, "Umm … Negative, commander. You're still dark."

"Do you want me to deploy the UAVs?" Emma offered. As mission specialist, she was the primary controller for all robotics on *Unity*. "I recommend a swarm scan."

"I concur. Start on the exterior." Varik crawled forward along the curved wall like a hamster in its wheel. "Send one to the openi—"

"Varik," Ishikawa cut in. "I see something."

Varik shielded himself with his arms and glanced back and forth, searching for whatever had alerted Ishikawa. "See what?"

"Turn off your light."

Despite the oddness of the request, Varik turned the dial on his helmet. The beam above his eyes dimmed and went dark. Janice and Ishikawa did the same, leaving nothing but . . .

He saw it. A dull, white glow was spilling out on the floor and ceiling from an indistinct doorway, one he might have passed by without noticing. A few puffs from his jetpack propelled him through the opening and across a catwalk that spanned a black pit. He turned his helmet lamp back on and shined it into the pooled shadows beneath him.

"I see coils of red metal below the bridge. It looks like the inside of a nautilus shell."

"Any idea what it might be for?" Nick asked.

"None." He didn't linger. Drawn by the gravity of his curiosity, Varik continued to the next door at the other end of the bridge. The source of the glow was inside the next room.

He barely made it past the door before halting, suspended in wonder. Nick spewed questions over the radio, but they reached Varik's ears as background noise. Pure, white light was radiating from a circular panel by the far wall. The glowing disc was tilted forward, displaying three shoebox-sized devices as if they were bracelets at a jeweler's shop. Rigid, wavy tubes hung from the ceiling above them like the roots of a tree.

The bizarre objects excited Varik, but not nearly as much as the recognizable blue holographs floating above the panel. Letters. The holographs were letters spelling out words from dozens of Earth languages. He could read several of them, and they all translated to the same message.

WITAM
CROESO
BIENVENIDO

WELCOME

#

"Are you guys ready?" Nick asked the crew, who had gathered around the comms display in *Unity*. He bit down on his lower lip, barely containing his smile, then the screen cut to black for a few seconds.

Here comes the big announcement, Varik thought.

The screen changed to a broadcast of Lynn Weiss, NASA's Public Affairs Officer, standing at a podium. The word live overlaid one corner of the display. Lynn was preparing her notes before addressing the media, and she looked excited enough to catapult off the stage like a rock star.

It had been a week since the crew's first collection mission on *Angel One*. They had sent their haul to Earth in a drop pod, including pieces of the ship's skin and gelatinous bags from beneath the floor. But Varik suspected the most significant item they took was the metal box, the one magnetically docked on the podium that projected holographic words.

The box had been linked to the other two by bundles of wires that resembled optical fibers. His years of experience in the Air Force and NASA told him such a device might be a flight recorder or processor.

An alien computer.

Cracking the processor's data would allow them to cheat off an advanced civilization's homework. What progress might scientists make in his lifetime? Interstellar travel? Communication with new worlds? Escape from Earth to healthier planets? Every problem from overcrowding to food shortages to potential extinction could be solved.

If landing on the moon was a giant leap, then *Unity*'s accomplishment was like soaring on an intercontinental flight.

On the monitor, Lynn Weiss grinned into a barrage of camera flashes and delivered her address.

"Ladies and gentlemen, as previously reported, the crew onboard *Unity* successfully harvested bags of an unknown substance from *Angel One* and sent them to Earth. The substance, popularly dubbed 'Soylent Green,' has been tested by NASA and the ESA, and both organizations came to the same conclusion. We can at this time confirm, with absolute certainty, the contents of the bags are a new species of algae.

"We have discovered life from another planet."

The reporters listening to Lynn stood and cheered. Likewise, the astronauts watching the announcement celebrated with unwieldy, floating hugs and high-fives. Ishikawa shook five grape juice pouches to add bubbles, then handed them out. Varik tapped his faux champagne against the others' and took a drink through his straw.

Lynn continued to announce more details from the discovery. "Astronaut Janice Widowicz offered some speculations about the purpose of the algae. She believes the builders of *Angel One* used it as a food source or intended to spread it on a planet as part of a terraforming effort—"

The communications monitor cut back to Nick. "You're all officially heroes. Janice, if I get my way, the new species will be named after you."

Janice brushed her drifting hair away from her face. She was blushing. "Thank you, but Widowicz doesn't sound so great in Latin."

"It does sound appropriately alien though." Callum nudged her with his elbow.

Janice laughed, then within the span of a blink, her enthusiasm hardened to concern. "The researchers are taking appropriate precautions, right?" she asked Nick.

"Yes, for the fourth time, I promise you they are. The research team is entirely isolated and unable to leave the facility within thirty days of having contact with the algae."

"Good. I'd hate to be the one responsible for introducing a deadly, latent virus on Earth."

"Don't worry. In fact, grab another drink. We have lots to celebrate. Babel?"

Varik perked up. "Yes?"

"You were right."

Varik gasped, and his crewmembers patted him on the back, dribbling him toward the floor. *The flight recorders.* "Are you saying what I think you are?"

Nick nodded and a burst of laughter popped out of his mouth. "Yep, it's a computer. And we've already tapped into it."

"No!" Varik exclaimed. His mouth hung agape.

"I kid you not. We can't read the data yet, and the machine is transmitting at an incredibly high rate. We're able to capture only a fraction of its output. But our engineers had the brilliant idea of searching for incrementing and reducing patterns of ten, like we saw when we first made contact. We found it. It's interlaced with other data, but the pattern is there."

Ishikawa pumped his arms, propelling his body into a spin.

Emma wiped away a tear with the palm of her hand. "We've really done it," she said. "We've heard from extraterrestrials."

Varik exhaled slowly as his mind and heart staggered under the weight of the news. "Do we have any idea how the ship knew to project greetings to us in multiple human languages?"

The display went dark before Nick could answer.

Varik blinked rapidly, pulled into mental focus by his reflection on the blank screen. Several of the astronauts called out to Nick, and Callum cycled power on the equipment. The connection with ground control did not recover.

Their joy got trampled as they scrambled from station to station. The crew urgently needed to determine the fault and regain communication with Earth. There were a thousand dangers that could kill an astronaut crew, and loss of comms meant being vulnerable to them. Varik hurried to the flight deck with

Callum and pulled up the ship's diagnostics on a monitor. His fingers sprinted over the screen, flicking from one box to the next.

"Anything?" he shouted down the ship's corridor. He received three different versions of "negative" as replies.

The issue had to be on *Unity*'s end, regardless of every system insisting in green it was functioning properly. NASA had more infrastructure redundancy than a small city, and even if it did go silent, the crew should have been able to contact the ESA, or JPL, or any bored kid tinkering with an amateur radio.

No one knew precisely when it happened, but during their frantic troubleshooting, an image appeared on the comms display. Varik noticed it first and called the rest of the crew into the module. The screen was displaying a satellite image of *Unity* orbiting above earth. No, not an image, because the lights on their ship were blinking. It was a video. It reminded Varik of the recordings he used to make while flying in formation with his wingmen. The camera angle was at the three o'clock high position.

Three o'clock high? Varik pushed back and climbed over Ishikawa and Callum as if they were rungs on a ladder. A thought had struck him like a fired bullet. Janice asked what he was doing, but he remained silent. He needed to look out the window, to dispel his concern. He hoped to see nothing but earth or stars.

No such luck. There it was, *Angel One*, drifting high and to the right, relative to their position. Varik shook his hand in front of the window and, on the comms display, saw himself waving from afar.

Someone was filming them from aboard *Angel One*. That realization would have been his greatest concern if not for the even more startling text that appeared on the screen, superimposed over the video. Varik's spine shivered as he read it.

HELLO VARIK.

HELLO UNITY.

#

Varik pulled his hand away from his mouth because of the burning sensation on the tip of his finger. He glanced down and saw he had been biting his nail, exposing the raw, pink flesh underneath. He kicked the habit years ago. When was the last time he gnawed them to the point of pain? During his divorce?

Most of the crew were once again floating around the monitor. Ishikawa, the exception, was strapped in at the nearby workbench as he built an override for the Direct Frequency Radio Controller. It had been forty hours since they last heard from anyone on earth. Forty hours since the entity supposedly aboard *Angel One* first reached out to them.

The stranger had been consistent in its pattern but sparse in details. Every ten hours, it broadcasted a live video feed of *Unity* and communicated via text on the ship's comms display. The crew could send messages to the stranger, who seemed pleased to answer trivial questions but avoided important ones by replying, "I AM GROUND CONTROL."

When they asked, "In what years did England win the World Cup?" the entity answered them.

1966 AND 2022.

"How did you learn English?"

FROM TRANSMISSIONS.

"Are you the one responsible for our communication issues?"

YES.

"Why?

I AM GROUND CONTROL

"Which star did you travel from?"

I AM GROUND CONTROL.

Despite the evidence, Varik found it hard to believe something aboard *Angel One* was severing their ground links. The crew ruled out hardware failures. Though doubtful, the hack might have come from Earth. Was an independent hacker group responsible, or perhaps Russia? The Roscosmos space agency would not endanger astronauts for revenge, but what about the Russian government?

Or Varik could accept the stranger's confession that the interference came from *Angel One*. After all, the logistics for an earthborn attack would have been incredibly complex, and the stranger's behavior was bizarre. Janice had suggested a distant stranger might be reaching out to them through *Angel One*, using it as a communications hub. Could she be right?

Callum twirled his weightless watch around his finger. "Two minutes," he said, referring to the time remaining until the entity would contact them again, assuming it maintained its pattern.

Varik rubbed the bridge of his nose. He had not slept in over two days and could feel the bags hanging beneath his eyes. "Ishikawa, how much longer for the radios?"

"I don't know." Ishikawa repositioned the vacuum nozzle he was using to collect smoke as he soldered a spacesuit computer to the radio controller. "It's hard to tell when McGuyvering a solution. A couple hours?"

"Keep it up. We need science to come to the rescue."

"Technically, it's engineering, not science," Ishikawa said through a yawn. "And Jan doesn't think science can save us anyway."

"What?" she exclaimed. "Ishikawa, I—" Janice shut her mouth and glared at him, as if he had betrayed her darkest secret.

"What do you mean?" Varik asked.

"Nothing," she said. "It's a long story."

"No, seriously. What do you mean?"

Varik sensed the other two were withholding a confession, and his patience was too frayed for anything but straight answers.

Speaking more angrily than he intended, he thrust a finger toward the floor and snapped, "You might as well tell me, because I can't talk to anyone down there."

Ishikawa opened his pursed lips and sighed. "She wasn't a fan of your speech. She said people can't be united by science."

The dull insult cut deeply into Varik's pride, partly because of his fatigue and respect for Janice, but mostly because the words he said aboard *Angel One* were supposed to be his immortal legacy.

"Well, what should I expect from someone who carries a crucifix in her pocket?"

Janice recoiled. "Hey! It's a reminder, not a magic charm. What I told him was that science is a method, not a moral cause. People don't rally around methodologies. They unite for causes like religion that are focused on people and greater meaning."

Varik scowled. "Religion uniting people? It's our leading cause of death."

"That's an old myth," Janice said with a dismissive flick of her hand. "Governments and diseases have killed far more people, but complex things are two-edged swords. They always have good and bad sides, and it's dishonest to admit to only one side and not the other. Bacteria cause plagues, but they're also essential for life. Governments cause wars but also protect people, and religions can serve the poor or serve themselves."

He had never heard this side of Janice before. "There's a reason I studied physics in school, not theology or philosophy. Too much bickering. Give me something that moves forward. Something that puts humans in space."

Janice rubbed one of her bloodshot eyes. She looked as tired as he felt. "It moves us forward in space, but not in ethics or civilization. It's morally neutral. Science creates bigger buildings but also bigger bombs. The greatest atrocities are usually committed by people with the technological advantage."

"But not in the name of science."

Janice crossed her arms. "I didn't hate your speech. All I said was that as wonderful as science may be, I think humans need more to unite. And science cuts both ways, just like religion and politics. It's usually beneficial, but if we blindly trust it, we fail to account for all of the variables and the end users. That's how tragedies occur."

"She's at least partly right," Ishikawa said without looking up from his work. "Technology made it possible for us to be here, but it also made it possible for us to be hacked."

Callum waved at them. "Can you finish debating later?" He pointed at the screen, which was displaying the exterior of *Unity*. "It's time."

Varik put aside his disagreement with Janice. Given that she moved close to watch the screen with him, it seemed she had put it aside as well. He said, "Ground Control, are you there?"

Callum typed the words and transmitted them.

After a few seconds, they received their response. YES. THIS IS GROUND CONTROL.

Varik dictated the conversation to Callum. "Ground Control, are you in *Angel One*, on Earth, or on a different planet?"

ALL.

"All?" Callum said. He wrinkled his nose at the answer as if it had a pungent stench.

Varik said, "Please explain. Are you on *Angel One* at this moment?"

YES.

"Where are you in the ship? We searched it several times."

Before Callum finished typing, the stranger replied, "I WAS WITH YOU, VARIK."

His pulse quickened and pumped ice through his veins. How did the stranger answer preemptively, and how did it know who was speaking? Could it hear them?

A new image replaced the video of *Unity*, one which caused Janice to clutch at her chest and stutter, "How? How?" The picture was a photograph of three astronauts in the dark corridors of *Angel One*. It had been taken from behind them and showed their jetpacks and helmets.

"Keep calm," Varik said, as much to himself as the others. He asked, "Are you human?"

I AM GROUND CONTROL.

Callum punched his left palm. "We're losing it again."

The "GROUND CONTROL" answers always preceded the stranger's hours of silence.

"Why are you doing this?" Varik asked.

The screen remained unchanged. Varik feared Callum was right about the conversation ending. However, after what felt like minutes, a new text appeared.

INTEGRATION WITH EARTH SYSTEMS COMPLETE. CONFINEMENT INITIATED.

A whirlwind of questions circled around the module as crewmembers asked each other what the message meant. Varik did not stay to hear their guesses. He was enraged by the stranger's mockery and haunted by the implications of "confinement," a word which conveyed no less dread than a death sentence. Varik flew out of the room and headed toward the airlock. Along the way, he grabbed a Taser gun. So much for peace.

He was halfway into his spacesuit when Callum called, "Commander, where are you?"

"I'm going over there and ending this."

"Really? What do you want us to do?"

Varik shoved his arm into his suit's sleeve. "Keep it busy. See what other information you can get."

Janice shouted, "I'm coming too."

Within minutes, the pair donned their suits and disembarked from *Unity*. Varik accelerated too quickly when he jetted toward the other ship. He had to correct his maneuvers to avoid tumbling and rotating.

A semi-transparent message appeared on Varik's visor display.

THIS IS GROUND CONTROL. VARIK AND JANICE, RETURN TO YOUR SHIP. PLANETARY CONFINEMENT IS REQUIRED.

Callum radioed, "Commander, I see a message."

"I see it too."

Screw confinement, Varik thought. *Angel One* was supposed to be their key to the stars, not a locked door. "Ground Control, stop interfering with our communications. We pose no threat."

RETURN TO YOUR SHIP. CONFINEMENT IS MANDATORY.

"No," Varik replied.

PROTECTION PROTOCOL INITIATED. SENTIENT LIFE FORM 46 RISK STATUS ELEVATED.

Should he go back to *Unity*? Did the entity know of other sentient species? Questions inundated Varik's mind, and chief among them was the one he asked Janice. "Is it an AI?"

"It's starting to sound like it," she said. "Varik, you need to slow down."

He was closing in with *Angel One* at a reckless speed. Varik reversed thrust in the final seconds, but his momentum was too high. He reached out to absorb the impact and slammed into the hull. Pain launched from his wrist and flew up his forearm. After his body bounced, he clutched the injury and sucked air through clenched teeth.

Janice screamed, "Varik!"

"I'm fine," he lied. His arm hurt, but at least it didn't feel broken. He needed to press on. When the ship opened a hole in its surface, he flew into the dark, gaping maw, then headed toward the holograph room.

RISK STATUS ELEVATED.

The warning blinked on Varik's display, but he didn't turn back. Then the stranger transmitted something new, a video broadcast from Earth. The British prime minister, who looked unusually disheveled, was addressing reporters in front of the Palace of Westminster.

"—Working to uncover the source of the computer virus. It's difficult because the effects have been widespread. Global, really."

She raised her chin as she listened to one of the reporters in the back, then said, "No, we don't know when railway service will be restored." After taking another question, she said, "We still suspect cyber terrorists. We have no evidence that suggests alien activity related to the *Unity* mission is at fault."

"We need to tell them," Varik said as he hustled clumsily through the curved hall. "Ishikawa, you need to hurry with those radios."

"Varik, which direction did you turn?" Janice asked.

"Meet me at the central chamber." He kept moving forward. After several seconds without a reply, he asked, "Janice?"

No one answered.

"Janice? Ishikawa?" Still no answer. "*Unity*?"

Communications with the ship and Janice were gone. He called each crewmember's name over his radio, but no one responded.

The only audio came from the news feed, where a man in a dark suit was running toward the prime minister. He stopped on the other side of the podium and whispered into her ear. Whatever he said caused her to open her eyes wide.

"I'm sorry," she mumbled into the microphone, then retreated to Westminster as quickly as her age and heels would allow. The reporters rioted with demands for information.

The video vanished. Varik heard nothing but the sound of his own heavy breathing. "Janice? Callum?"

What was going on? Their situation felt like it had just veered in a new, terrible direction, but toward what?

He was about to stop and go back in search of Janice when a glowing message appeared in the corner of his visor's HUD. The simple statement struck him with ominous, indifferent finality.

THIS IS GROUND CONTROL.
PROCESS IS COMPLETE.

He needed to go on, to put an end to this madness quickly. The doorway to the holograph room was near. Varik clawed his way toward it, even with his injured arm. His suit's cooling system activated, blowing sweat off his brow. "Stop this, Ground Control."

REDUCING RISK LEVEL.

Anger and fear wrestled in his chest as he reached the bridge to the holograph room. "Stand down, Ground Control," he ordered, unsure of how to de-escalate the situation.

WELCOME BACK, VARIK.

He flew into the room, which appeared unchanged since the last time he saw it. The tilted pedestal glowed beneath the two remaining processors. It projected various forms of "Welcome" into the air.

A section of curved wall illuminated and projected the view of Earth from outside *Angel One*. They were on the dark side of the planet. Varik recognized the western half of North America by the pattern of glowing cities.

"Where are you, Ground Control?" he shouted.

The blue holographs scattered into a swarm of dots, then coalesced into three arrows.

Two pointed at the processors on the lighted pedestal, and the other pointed at Earth.

I AM HERE. INTEGRATION COMPLETE.

The stranger was an AI, or rather a virus, and it had been hiding in the computer he sent to Earth. He had infected NASA and, based on the news broadcast, countless other systems across the globe. Guilt tore through him like a grenade blast. He trembled, causing his rapid breath to stutter.

CONFINEMENT IS MANDATORY. SENTIENT LIFE FORM IS TO REMAIN ON ITS PLANET.

This can't be. His discovery was supposed to be Earth's future, their ticket to the stars.

DO YOU LIKE FIREWORKS, VARIK?

The question confused and terrified him. Fireworks?

The dimming view of Earth dragged Varik's attention to the wall display. Cities went black, turning the planet into a dark orb. Then, as he watched in paralyzed horror, the silent fireworks show began. A burst of light appeared from the area where Las Vegas had been glowing seconds before. Then Phoenix. Then cities up and down the Pacific coast.

Varik realized what the new phase of the AI's plan was. He begged for it to stop, but his voice merely echoed inside his helmet. His heart plummeted into a black hole of sickening dread.

The circles of light continued to flash at random across Earth's surface. The devastating nuclear explosions coruscated like fireflies on a moonless night.

The End

C.W. Briar

C.W. "Chuck" Briar writes fantasy and science fiction with a touch of traditional horror. He loves stories that make him think and smile while also creeping him out. His first book, Wrath and Ruin, is a collection of stories from a variety of genres. His next book, *Whispers from the Depths*, is a dark fantasy novel with heavy Viking influences and water magic. It will release in 2019.

Briar is a systems engineer with a background in trains and aircraft. He graduated from Binghamton University and is also a certified apologist through Biola University. He lives in Upstate NY with his wife, kids, and corgi pack.

www.cwbriar.com

Seeking What's Lost

Cindy Koepp

J'Nia glanced over Horizon Systems' contest rules one more time. A useless effort, really. She'd had the rules memorized five days ago. Her AI-run scenario controller and characters met the requirements for the contest as much as they had when she'd written the programs. Just one last test for real-time mode, and her "feral bear" would be ready to send in before the midnight deadline.

She glanced at the clock. *Almost nine o'clock already? Get a move on, woman!*

J'Nia walked into her home office, her sanctuary where she programmed game scenarios and sought solace. A mural of her children playing with red, green, and blue balloons decorated the wall ahead of her. The two walls to her sides were lined with mementos. To the right, stuffed animals, an assortment of dolls, and a baseball and glove adorned the glossy white shelves. Cartoon characters, fridge-worthy drawings, and a flannel quilt of pastel blue occupied the more rustic, raw wood shelves to her left. This shrine to her lost children brought bittersweet recollections of the events that made each piece special.

They would have been eight and six now. Someday, she'd make her own trip to heaven and be reunited with her children. In the meantime, this room brought back both happier memories and her greatest grief. Many of her friends said she needed to redecorate and move on, and maybe, if God blessed her with more children, she might someday. For now, though, the meager comfort it provided would be enough. She smiled and ran her hand along the blue quilt then caressed a doll. Her sweet babies had been stolen from her too soon. She balled up a fist and scowled. What kind of sick lowlife killed children?

Chill. Get the playtest done.

She unclenched her fists and picked up her gear. The VR helmet and gloves fit like they belonged there and powered on as soon as they were settled in place. Her opening screen took form like random puzzle pieces that filled in around her a few at a time until she had a full three-dimensional view. The walls of her virtual room were lined with rows of drawers, each labeled with the name of a program.

When she opened the one marked "Jael," the room turned into glitter and reformed as a cave.

The system pinged. Welcome, Jael. Please choose a play mode.

A slider appeared numbered from one for turn-based to five for real-time. She picked five, a mode for experts in which the computer would not prompt her with ideas, helps, or clues. If combat happened, she'd have to stay on her toes. The computer wouldn't wait for her to decide on an action.

Please select the number of desired quests.

A cursor blinked at the end of the text.

As a rule, each quest was supposed to take about an hour of playing time, give or take. She could squeak in two quests and still have a bit of time to spare.

The system pinged twice, and a message bar slid down from the top of the image.

Quest: Find missing cubs.

Quest: Feed all three bears.

Seeking What's Lost

Find the missing cubs?

Her breath caught. The headlines from three years ago were still too clear in her mind. By the time the police had caught the kidnappers, the Amber Alerts had spanned the country.

J'Nia shook her head. This was a silly game. For whatever reason, the AI had chosen to have the cubs wander off. Coincidence. Nothing more. Surely the scenario controller wouldn't have turned a tragedy from her real life into a game scenario for her to play.

Mental note: Next time, give the AI more direction. She considered restarting the game to get a new quest. No. I'll find these cubs. It's just a game. Be the bear. Finish the quest.

Jael rolled onto her side, stood in place, and turned. Unlike the turn-based mode, which made sixteen-point turns, in real-time, the image rotated smoothly with no graphic trash or jitters. The crystals in the gray rock glittered in the beam of sunlight that broke the gloom. Wind-blown pine needles littered the floor in weird clumps that filled the depressions. When she faced the opening, the sky shined through.

Jael blew out a breath and lumbered forward. Her joints creaked as she limbered up from her nap. Once outside, she blinked in the mottled shade of the tree canopy until her eyes adjusted. The pine trees grew straight and tall. Claw marks scarred the dark, rough bark on a few of them where she'd left her mark. High in the trees, songbirds chirped, and squirrels chased each other across the branches. Reddish brown pine needles covered the ground.

The ground showed no pawprints. There was one bare patch where pine needles had been scraped aside. The cubs might have indulged in a brief wrestling match. Very brief, judging from the size of the scuff. Other than that, her cubs hadn't left her a physical trail to follow. Gone without a trace, like three years ago. She blinked back tears.

It's a game. Just finish the quest, and the next time, don't have the AI get quest ideas from old news reports.

Jael pushed off and stood on her back feet. Tall pine trees and stunted brush surrounded her, but no cubs were visible. She flopped to all fours and sniffed the ground. Gray, transparent words swam across the screen.

Oba, Dina, three different squirrels, pine trees, fresh berries

She walked forward, twisting her head from side to side and shouldering her way through the loose parts of the brush. Twigs briefly caught in her fur but pulled loose as she pushed onward.

The squirrels dropped off the screen after a few steps. Oba and Dina were joined briefly by a few woodpeckers and chipmunks, but Jael ignored the smaller wildlife and continued on after her own children.

Cubs. Cubs, not children.

To get her mind off the old wound in her heart, Jael focused on the terrain, admiring the details. An iridescent beetle crawled across her path. Hard knocks heralded a woodpecker searching for dinner. Gradually, the brush thinned, and the tree canopy became more sparse.

Nearby, water crashed over rocks. The scent trail led to a bluff overlooking a fast-moving stream. River-washed stones shined in greens, purples, grays, and tans that had darker and lighter speckles. Quartz veins glittered in the sandstone. Grasses waved in the wind. A bee buzzed as it flew past her ear. The transparent text showing what she could smell revealed Oba and Dina along with four wolves, a squirrel, and two deer. Twenty-feet below, the water rushed by, turning white and foamy.

Here's hoping those cubs haven't gone for a swim.

Surely they weren't crazy enough to take a flying leap into rapids. She'd programmed them with more intelligence and self-preservation than that, hadn't she? Jael scouted around to find the strongest scent of her cubs or physical clues about the way they'd gone from here.

The message bar at the top turned red.

Feral Wolf Pack detected. Hostile.

Four scrawny wolves with patchy fur left the trees and growled. All four showed green health bars fully lit up. The quartet slinked forward growling and baring their teeth. One, a paler gray than the others, took the lead with three smaller, darker wolves flanking. She could probably run for it. Bears could really cover ground when they felt the need. Over thirty miles per hour according to her research for this project, but if the cubs were still nearby, the wolves would undoubtedly go after them next. She should be able to take on four mangy wolves. The cubs? Probably not. She'd deal with this threat, unlike the "wolves" she hadn't known about soon enough three years ago. To think she'd once dated that jerk.

Too far away for an attack, Jael darted forward several steps, clacking her teeth and blowing out a breath. She narrowed her eyes and flattened her ears against her head. If these wolves wanted a fight, they'd found the bear to give them one.

The wolf pack charged forward, two darker ones circling and the others closing the rest of the distance between them and coming into melee range.

She reared back and whacked the pale wolf across the face with her huge paw. The wolf spun away and landed with its feet in the air. The health bar dropped halfway and turned yellow. A second wolf charged at her, and she slapped it into a small boulder. The health bar dropped to one quarter and went red. The other two wolves passed out of her peripheral vision.

Either the first wolf I hit was the pack's alpha, or I got a really bad damage roll the first time.

She turned toward the flanking pair. Those two wolves each went for a bite attack. One missed even though Jael hadn't moved that leg.

Critical failure. Stinks to be you.

The other bit her leg. Real pain passed to J'Nia via an electrical jolt.

Jael leaned over for a bite to the wolf's neck, but her teeth closed on nothing when the wolf let go and retreated far enough. Her own health bar dropped a few points.

Jael hit the two nearest wolves with a broad sweep of her paws. Both spun away. One dropped into red on the health bar. The other zeroed out.

Critical hit! Good going, bear. Now let's take out the others.

She spun back around. The two wolves she'd struck the first time charged back into range. The stronger of the two bit her leg, sending a jolt through the VR glove, then darted back. Jael lost more health points. The other crouched to get ready to pounce. Jael drew back, prepared to teach that wolf to fly.

She swung her claws at the closer wolf but missed when it ducked. The crouching one leapt. She swept her arm across. It yelped when she hit it and spun away and died. That left the alpha and one other.

The alpha crouched for a jump. Jael twisted and swatted downward, slamming the alpha into the rocks. Its health bar zeroed out. She turned to the last as it circled her, crouched low, and growled. Jael pivoted to track the wolf. She struck the ground and huffed. The wolf flinched and darted back a few steps before it resumed circling. After a couple more steps, the wolf launched toward Jael. She smacked the wolf into next week with a swipe of her paw. The bar still showed a couple red pixels, but bleeding would take care of that momentarily.

Hmm. Too easy. Four wolves and I barely got a couple health dings.

She called up the options screen and scrolled to the **Combat Difficulty** slider. It was currently set at about thirty percent. That would balance the battles in her favor. Given her time constraints that probably wasn't a bad idea. A higher level meant the battles took longer and needed more recovery time, but walkthroughs were boring. She shrugged and nudged the slider a bit over halfway then closed the screen.

The system pinged.

Level Up

Slap, Dodge, and Bluff Charge skills increased. Smell attribute increased.

Eat corpses? Yes/No

Eww, gross! No.

In most games J'Nia had played, the monsters vanished after the battle unless they had something important she needed. These didn't, but when she searched a corpse, she got the same prompt about dining on wolf meat. Fortunately, the stock images from Horizon Systems' art department didn't show much realistic gore, since Horizon Systems had rated this version of the game engine for All Audiences. The wolves had a patch of red on their fur, but nothing more gruesome than that.

J'Nia shuddered, which translated to Jael shaking like a bathed hound. She sniffed the alpha wolf but picked up no scent of her cubs.

As she turned her attention back to the ground, transparent gray words swam across the screen:

Oba, Dina, freshwater, wet dirt, fish, two different male humans, donkey

Humans? Did they take the cubs?

Jael picked up her pace. Each step with her wounded leg gave her a mild shock. Her health meter showed about eighty percent, so she pushed on. Jael left the ravine behind and headed back into the pine trees, watching for physical sign her cubs had been this way. Hummingbirds flittered around a tree covered by a dark green, viny plant with purple, trumpet-shaped flowers. The rocky cliff loomed ahead of her. Her den was to the south. A gaping opening in the rock beckoned. As she drew nearer, pale streaks on a pine tree's bark drew her eye. The thin, short streaks came in sets of five, spaced just right for Oba's or Dina's paws.

The cubs had been here and climbed a tree, probably to escape the humans. Jael paused and sniffed around the tree. No blood, either human or bear, but the human scent came through more strongly here. They'd stayed for some time, probably waiting for the cubs to come down, maybe even trying to get them down.

Her heart pounded.

If you two hurt my children, I'll–

When the law had finally caught up to the twits who'd taken her own children, her real children, she'd parked outside the jail with a .38 revolver in her purse and a determination to get as close as she had to, waiting for the chance that had never come. An officer in her tiny town had recognized her and called her husband. Israel had managed to convince her, somehow, to leave the matter of justice with the law. Getting her own revenge would have only satisfied her rage briefly, and then she'd be in jail. That would not have brought her kids back.

Yeah, that was all logical. It all made sense, but she still wondered – often at two in the morning when she couldn't sleep – if she'd made the right choice. Maybe she shouldn't have let her husband talk her out of her bit of frontier justice. As it was, the legal system's idea of justice would have the murderers out on parole a few years from now. Her innocent babies, in contrast, had gotten a death sentence. How was that in any way fair? This time, there were no small-town police, and Israel wouldn't care if she massacred a whole city here. The jerks who had stolen her cubs were as good as dead.

Jael ran, following the scent to a cave, one further north than the den where she and her cubs slept. When she faced the cave, the names of her cubs shrank but stayed on the screen. The humans and donkey were joined by a new entry: rotten meat. Clearly, her cubs had been here, but were they still around? Were they still alive?

"Figure that's enough pelts?" one human asked.

Further inside the cave, wood creaked.

"I think we've got room for a couple more. Some people will pay a lovely price for bear pelts, and we know there's at least one more around here," a second human answered.

"Where there are cubs … "

You hurt my cubs?

Jael ran into the cave. The blood and half-rotted meat crowded out most of the transparent text on the screen. The scents of the two men and donkey faded to tiny, nearly invisible text. The donkey hitched to a wagon brayed and backed away.

"Whoa! Whoa! What's wrong with Sadie?" the second human asked.

Jael rose up on her back feet. The two men both showed full green bars. They were in the back of the shallow cave, piling pelts and barrels on the wagon. Both men were tall and lean. One had a weathered face and grayer hair. The other had a gaunt face and narrow eyes.

A red banner appeared at the top of the image.

Two humans. Hunters. Hostile.

"Axa, get my gun," the older human said.

As Axa reached for a black-powder musket, Jael dropped to all fours again. With her seven hundred pounds of bulk blocking the only way out, they wouldn't run. She had no chance of scaring them away, and she was pretty sure even bears couldn't dodge bullets, so she charged into range.

Axa had grabbed the gun by the time Jael arrived. She slapped both men, sending the older one back against the wall with a full quarter of his health gone. Axa's gun smacked into the wall and clattered on the rock floor. His health meter only fell a few points.

The older human got back to his feet and drew a long-bladed knife. The men were too far apart to attack both at once, but the musket would take time to load, so she turned to the knife-wielding human. As he closed in with the knife aimed at her gut, Jael dodged the knife thrust and swiped with both massive paws. The human fell back and lost another chunk of health points. The knife bounced under the wagon. The human reached for it but came up far too short. Jael looked back at Axa. He had recovered the musket and was digging in a hip pouch for something.

Jael left him for the moment and returned to the older human. He'd picked up a stick with a metal point at the end and jabbed it at her. Her attempt to dodge failed, and the point scored a minor nick on her leg. The second time, she swiped at it and knocked it aside before stepping in to deliver a solid whack that took the rest of the human's health.

She spun back to the other human. Axa fumbled with a ramrod, then dropped it and brought the musket up to his shoulder. Jael charged into range and batted the barrel of the gun aside as Axa fired. A loud pop preceded an even louder bang and the word "gunpowder" sprawled across the screen obliterating other scent words. A high-pitched hum overrode the other ambient sounds. Jael slapped as hard as she could and sent the human bouncing first off the corner of the crate, then off a wall before he hit the ground like a bag of rocks. Half his health points were instantly gone.

As he recovered, she closed the gap. Axa produced a long, heavy-bladed knife and slashed with it. She jerked aside and got a thin slice across her arm. The electrical jolt made her flinch. She lashed out with the other paw, dropping the human's health to zero. The system pinged.

Partial Hearing Loss -5 for Two Hours. Partial Smell Loss -15 for Two Hours.

Eat Corpses? Yes/No

Jael selected No. The corner of J'Nia's eyes burned as she and rummaged through the cave, overturning crates and tossing wolf pelts and deer hides. A fuzzy, dark pelt peeked out from under a crate. The pelt's color was a good match for Dina, but too dark for Oba. Jael trembled as she pushed the crate aside to find the pelt was shaped like a scrawny wolf.

She blew out a breath and willed her tense muscles to relax. Her cubs weren't here. She looked back at the dead humans and sank to all fours. She'd killed them without cause. They hadn't hurt her kids, but perhaps they would have.

Could she really justify attacking people who could or even might hurt her kids? That hardly seemed right.

It's a game. It's just a game. It was part of the quest, not some heavy moral dilemma. Focus on solving the quests. Jael left the cave and sat. *Now, where are those cubs? Sniffing them out is taking half an eternity! What other skills do I have that might do me some good?*

She called up the stat screen.

Recent changes in italics.	
Name: Jael **Class:** Feral, *Level 2*	**Species:** Ursid – Grizzly **Gender:** Female
Attributes:	
Power: *86* **Speed:** 28 **Charm:** 25 **Vitality:** 65 ***Hearing:*** *65/70 1:36:32* ***Health:*** *164/244*	**Cleverness:** 53 **Endurance:** 58 **Agility:** 21 **Sight:** 30 ***Smell:*** *45/60 1:36:32* **Encumbrance:** 143
Skills:	

Primary: ***Slap:*** *27* **Bite:** 23 ***Dodge:*** *24* **Forage:** 33 **Track:** *22*	**Secondary:** **Trek:** 15 **Sprint:** 15 ***Bluff Charge:*** *28* **Intimidation:** 27 ***Charge:*** *21*
Other: **Sneak:** 15 **Problem Solving:** 12 **Hibernate:** 20	

Most of her primary skills were combat-oriented. Of the two that weren't, her cubs didn't qualify as food or shelter, so that left foraging out. The tracking skill was pretty puny. Her secondary skills were equally no good for the current task. The "Other" skills?

Hey, I'll just hibernate, and maybe they'll return to me in my dreams. She rolled her eyes and snickered. *Yeah, if only. Okay, so Smell it is.*

Her health was down a full third and still declining slowly but steadily. The little shocks from her glove with each step of her injured legs were getting irksome. She ought to rest, but as long her chil – her cubs were missing, she wouldn't be stopping.

Jael sniffed around the area. "Gunpowder" took the bulk of the screen, overwriting the other faint text. As the words shifted around with her movement, some of the others became clear, but only for a moment. Several minutes of walking revealed the rest of the text.

Rxxted mext, pxnx neexxes, dxnkxx, 2 hxmxns, mxxx, Xba, Dixx

The blocked letters were meant to represent the temporary loss of smell. Reasonable, but she'd seen most of that text before. "Xba" was undoubtedly "Oba," and "Dixx" had to be Dina.

The trail turned back toward the stream. The trees weren't nearly so tall, and brush took over as the main feature of the terrain. The sound of rushing water became louder. Vines with the purple trumpet flowers covered the trees and shrubbery, providing space for hummingbirds and bumblebees. If she had time, she'd explore, admire the scenery. Some other time, maybe. She had to get a move on.

As she walked, her health meter slowly declined. Those injuries, minor though they were, would continue to cost her more than she could afford to lose. In Horizon Systems' games, there were three ways to deal with injuries: take a nap; eat some food; or find a human with healer, herbalist, or physician skills. She had yet to meet any friendly humans in this AI-generated scenario. Was that a fault she should fix before submitting the game to Horizon Systems' contest? Did it really matter in a scenario this short? If there was time, she'd address that when she finished. For now, her wounded grizzly had kids to find.

Jael stopped and sat down both to review her options and to get a break from the complaints of her gloves. A nap would take too long. Even a few hours' sleep in real-time mode would put her past the contest deadline. She hadn't run into any healers in this scenario. That left food. The only food options she'd seen so far were the wolf carcasses and the humans she'd just killed. The wolves were too far away, and she had no interest in eating humans. Eat the donkey?

That meant another fight, and with her health approaching half already, that might not be a good idea. One critical hit from a donkey's rear kick, and she'd be one dead bear. No thanks.

With her sense of smell temporarily reduced, she didn't like her chances of sniffing out berries.

Jael huffed. She'd keep her eyes peeled and keep following the scents. She was headed toward the stream. Depending on how hard fishing was, she might be up for some ultra-fresh sashimi.

She followed the scent of "Xba" and "Dixx" to a shallow spot in the stream. Quartz veins in the sandstone shined in the sunlight. The water-washed rocks came in a greater variety of colors and shapes than the ravine downstream. The stones at the edge were still wet further away than could be explained by simple splashing. Had the cubs been this way recently?

Her health bar turned yellow when it hit halfway. Cubs would have to wait.

Large fish leapt out of the water, heading upstream. Jael waded out to the middle. Cool water rushed past her legs, stinging the bites and cuts she'd received. She waited for a fish to jump. As soon as it left the water, she lunged and snapped her jaws. The first effort missed altogether. The second fish slapped her nose with its tail as it flew by. She tried several more times before her teeth sank into one.

Eat corpse? Yes/No

This time she picked Yes.

Tasty!

Yeah, maybe, but needs more wasabi and ginger.

Half her health points were restored. Catching a second one took about the same number of tries but restored her points to full. The hum faded a little but still drowned out some of the ambient noise. She sniffed around on the far side of the stream. Gunpowder no longer crowded out everything.

4 huxxns – 3 malxs, 1 fexxle, Oba, Dinx, Humxn fxod, wxlf, x specxxs of xirdx

Sense of smell is improving, judging from the number of missing letters.

A whine, like a scared dog, came from somewhere nearby. Rising over that, children laughed. That might be the wolf she'd scented, or it could be her cubs. She recalled the video of that final showdown between the police and her control freak ex-boyfriend and his perpetually high buddy. One of them – each had blamed the other – had killed both of her precious babies before the police had arrived. The courts had decided to place the blame on the drug addict, but her money was still on her ex. He'd threatened her and her family enough times in the nine years after she'd married Israel. She'd even gotten a restraining order, for all the good that had done.

Jael ran on ahead, following the sounds as much as the scents. As she left the stream, the wolf scent faded. The land rose in a sandy dune with sparse vegetation.

As she crested the ridge, she found two cubs, one darker than the other, backed against a rock formation by two human boys, both wielding driftwood sticks like spears. They took turns driving the point at the cubs and stopping short.

The banner at the top turned red.

4 humans – 2 boys. Hostile. 2 adults. Unknown.

Leave my kids alone!

Jael ran forward half the distance and bared her teeth. The two boys screamed and dropped their sticks. She raced toward her cubs' attackers, snarling. Both bear cubs retreated to Jael as fast as their little legs could go.

Two adult humans came over the next dune. The female called the kids to her while the male picked up a chunk of driftwood, holding it like a baseball bat.

Jael stopped and clacked her teeth. The humans stood their ground. She ran half the distance then slapped the ground. Her cubs' tormentors reached their mother.

The woman pushed her children behind her but held onto them. "Galen, let's go. She's got cubs, and that stick won't stop her if she's feeling threatened."

Galen backed up a few steps and held onto the stick. The children peeked around their mother.

Jael huffed and struck the ground with her paw again.

The humans turned and ran, but the banner stayed red. The cubs caught up and stayed behind her. She raced after the humans, determined to make sure they were no threat to her cubs ever again. Jael was closing the distance fast when one of the boys tripped over a half-buried hunk of wood.

"Mama!" he hollered.

Jael stopped. Her own children used to call for her like that when they had scraped a knee or gotten a splinter. Could she really strike down these children? Even in a game?

Jael glanced back at her cubs, running to catch up to her again. They looked fine, though she'd have to do a more thorough check later. No. She wouldn't kill the humans. They needed to go away, definitely, but killing the children would make her no better than the murderers of her own. Leaving them orphaned wasn't any more acceptable.

The man picked up the boy who'd fallen and carried him as they continued on at a flat-out sprint, leaving a red and white plaid cloth and a basket behind.

Once the humans had retreated out of range, the system pinged several times.

Quest Complete: Find missing cubs.

Level Up

Bluff Charge and Foraging skills increased.

Attributes restored.

Jael looked back at her cubs, tumbling over each other in the sand, and led them to the picnic laid out nearby.

The system pinged again.

You have found a cache of human food. Feed cubs? Yes/No

She chose Yes and got another ping as the two adorable fluffballs stuffed roasted chicken in their faces.

Quest Complete: Feed all three bears.

All quests complete. Continue playing? Yes/No

J'Nia picked No, and the game returned her to her starting room. After logging out, she took off her equipment and sniffled.

Not bad really, unfortunate reminders of her grief notwithstanding. Was there time to add a few lines of code to prevent the AI from pulling more scenarios like that one? She checked the digital clock and tapped her finger on the desk. With an hour and a half to go, she had time to go tweak the AI then run a single quest to playtest it, but was that worth her time and effort?

Computerized bear cubs couldn't replace her own flesh and blood, but for just a moment the AI had allowed her to do in the game what she'd been too late to do in real life: rescue her children.

No. She'd leave the AI scenario controller alone.

J'Nia surfed to Horizon Systems' website and uploaded her contest entry.

The End

Cindy Koepp

Originally from Michigan, Cindy Koepp combined a love of pedagogy and ecology into a 14-year career as an elementary science specialist. After teaching four-footers -- that's height, not leg count -- she pursued a Master's in Adult Learning with a specialization in Performance Improvement. Her published works include science fiction and fantasy novels, a passel of short stories, and a few educator resources. When she isn't reading or writing, Cindy is currently working as a tech writer, hat collector, quilter, crafter, and crazy African Grey wrangler.

Recalled from the Red Planet

C.O. Bonham

I'm writing this from my bunk aboard the space ship Persephone as it drags me toward Earth, a planet I have never walked on. And away from the only home I have ever known. As you're probably aware, Mars has been abandoned and all citizens are returning to Earth. You may know the official tag line, Humanity Reunited, but you can't begin to comprehend the truth until you hear my story.

My name is Mark and if you're reading this then you are one of the many who are wondering what in the solar system is going on. Well, every story has a beginning. The history books are filled with stories about the colonization of Mars, but this is the first I know of that's written about its end.

We do things on Mars differently than on Earth. First of all we don't have toilet paper. "Inconceivable," you say? Well, we're shocked that Earthlings would waste a valuable resource like trees to wipe yourselves. Haven't you converted to suction toilets yet?

We also all get along. We are all Martians. We have no room for conflict; one crisis could be the last. If the crops fail, we all die. If a dome wall is punctured, we all die. If one person decides their ego is more important than pulling for the team, we all die. It means we don't let our differences define our friendships.

Like Justin and I. Justin was a Christian, but he wasn't all preachy or, "You have to be saved." He accepted that bugging me about going to church was only going to annoy me. I accepted that his beliefs were not a threat to me. It wasn't a huge gulf between us or even a taboo subject; we had some pretty good debates about it from time to time.

The most memorable debate was the one that changed my life. We finished class and were walking the crystalline tunnels between domes. "So do you want to come by and have supper? We could study, too."

Justin shrugged his light shoulder bag higher up. "Normally I would, but I can't tonight. I signed up for a Bible Prophesy class."

"Bible Prophesy?" I asked. "I thought that archaic tome was about ancient history. If the Bible really foretold the future, then don't you think it would mention the Mars colony or even space travel in general?"

Justin thought about it and every once in a while he would utter a "but" or an "uh" but he never managed to complete a thought.

"What's this? Speechless? I guess I finally won a debate."

Justin finally managed, "Me not having an answer is not a debate. I am sure it has to be in there somewhere. Why don't you come with me, and we can ask Reverend Travers?"

Reverend Travers was not only the spiritual leader for the community, but he was also an astronomer and a meteorologist. I liked the Rev but to be honest it made my ego cringe to think of talking to him about a religious question. What if he wasn't as stumped as Justin?

"Sorry, I have to get home, or my dad won't have supper. Besides it's going to take me all night to do this physics homework."

"True," he said and grinned. "I'll ask anyway and let you know what he says."

"Okay, you do that."

"Catch you later." He veered off into another hallway.

I was pretty pleased about stumping him. My happiness was short-lived though.

#

"Hey Mark!" Justin came up behind me on my way to our Saturday morning communications shift.

I fell into step beside him. "Hi, ready to declare me the winner yet?"

"First, it wasn't a debate. Second, I talked with the Rev, and he showed me some verses that kind of sound like they're about people in space."

We reached the communications room, and I scanned my ID to gain entry. "They 'kind of sound?' Everything in the Bible has like fifty million ways to interpret it. So how can 'kind of sound' be good evidence?"

The crew we were relieving was already standing and ready to exit. Justin and I pulled out our chairs and sat down at our consoles, ready to respond if any urgent messages came in.

"Listen to the verses and try to think them out, you might see where I'm coming from."

"Fine."

"Deuteronomy, chapter thirty verse four: Even if you have been banished to the most distant land under the heavens, from there the Lord will gather you."

I scratched my head. "Okay I listened and I can still think of at least fifty ways to interpret it. What makes you think it refers to Mars?"

"Because the only people in space right now are us, unless you count ISS and Lunar outpost three."

"They're more in space than we are. At least we have an atmosphere above us."

"Yes, but they can get to earth in a day. It would take us months. Face it—we are 'banished to the most distant land under the heavens.'"

"True, but the verse is clearly talking about Earth's sky, not space. After all, it was written *thousands* of years ago. There's no way it could apply to us."

"What about John ten sixteen? 'I have other sheep that are not of this pen. I must bring them also.' We are definitely not of Earth; both of us were born here on Mars. You have to admit, nothing says different pen more than a separate planet."

"Come on Justin, planets are not pens. And people are not sheep."

Justin started to say something else, but he got interrupted by an incoming transmission. We continued to stay busy for the rest of our shift and couldn't talk about it anymore.

He went the rest of the week without mentioning it again. We did our homework together and we watched movies together but neither of us would broach the subject. This would have been fine because as far as I was concerned, I'd finally won. But for some reason I really wanted to know why he was willing to let this go. Justin wasn't a sore loser, but he never accepted defeat easily. Especially on a religious point.

#

Friday night, I waited outside the module where Justin's Bible class met. I knew he wouldn't have plans afterward because he always went home to start dinner for his mom after she got finished at the infirmary.

"Finally. You guys talk forever."

"Hey Mark, What are you doing here?"

"I finished my homework. A new record," I lied.

"Cool. So do you want to come back to my place and hang out for a while?"

"That's what I'm here for."

#

Justin's pod looked the same as my pod and every other one on Mars. There was a viewing screen with a small sitting area on the far wall. To the right of the door, a small counter projected from the wall with a ration storage cabinet and the rehydrator, which looked like an old-fashioned microwave, mounted above. Bathroom on the right and bedrooms on the left.

Justin got us some drinks while I placed a prepackaged entrée into his rehydrator. When he sat down, I broached the subject.

"You remember our shift in the radio room last Saturday?"

"Yeah. Why?"

"Do you remember what you were going to say before you were interrupted?"

"Wow! I never expected you to ask. Before I got interrupted, I was gonna start into the book of Revelations and talking about the end times and the Rapture. Honestly, I was relieved when that call came in because I didn't know how you would react. I mean even some Christians try to avoid the subject."

"So talk about it now. If you have words to speak, I have ears to hear you. Or something like that."

"Yeah something like that." Justin grinned. "Okay so there was one more verse. 'And he will select his angels and gather his elect from the four winds, from the ends of the earth to the ends of the heavens.' It's from the gospel of Mark, chapter thirteen, verse twenty-seven. This one mentions both the Earth and the Heavens, but I didn't bring it up because unlike the first two verses it's about the Rapture."

"And what is the Rapture?"

"At the end of time Jesus Christ is going to return and take all of his followers to heaven with him. And then everyone who didn't accept him as their savior will be left behind for a period of judgments. During this time a world leader will emerge and declare himself a god on Earth."

"Will this be soon or something?" the rehydrator dinged and I reached in to pull out the meal.

"No one knows when Jesus will return. Christians have been waiting for him to come for thousands of years now. But when it happens, the Bible says it will happen fast. Specifically, it says it will be in the twinkling of an eye. Two men are together and then, one is gone."

"Okay, now you are starting to creep me out."

"Sorry but that's why I never brought it up. I didn't want to scare you away by getting all preachy."

"It's alright. I asked. Sometimes I forget how much your faith is a part of you."

"Sometimes I forget too. But it really does mean everything to me. Being a Christian isn't just a Sunday morning ritual. It's a way of living. And after Dad died it became a promise that Mom and I would see him again." Justin paused for a minute and picked up his data pad. "Here take this home with you. You don't have to read it, if you don't want to" He lit the screen and opened an app from the homepage.

"Um, sure, I guess it wouldn't hurt. Thanks." I stammered, running my fingers over the screen. It read: HOLY BIBLE. The page flicked and the heading, "Genesis Chapter one," appeared.

"If you want to read more, download it to yours. If you don't care then ignore it. Either way you can you return it tomorrow, when we go on radio duty. Okay?"

"Sounds good."

Justin's mom walked in, "Well, hi Mark. are you staying for supper?"

It wasn't often I would refuse an offer of food but I felt awkward, I needed time to process our discussion. "Sorry, no. I already ate with my dad." Another lie. Dad was working late.

#

That night I flipped back and forth between the open app on Justin's pad and my abandoned homework.

I did not read the Bible straight through-- I flipped around and took in different parts. Was I buying it as history? Not really. It was too weird. Too many inconsistencies. But it was fascinating from a mythological perspective.

I looked at the size of the app and decided it wasn't worth the space. My curiosity was sated. I would return his pad tomorrow and our friendship would go back to the way it'd always been.

If only.

#

The next morning I grabbed both data pads and headed down to the radio station.

I met Justin in our usual corridor and passed off his data pad to him.

"So did you get a chance to check it out?" he asked.

"Yeah some, it was interesting, but so large I kept flipping around and getting lost."

"Did you download it?"

His face held such an air of expectation, I almost wanted to say I did to keep him from being disappointed in me. "No, I couldn't justify the storage space." My words sounded lame to my own ears, and judging by the way Justin's face fell, I guessed it sounded lame to his, too.

We entered the radio station and took over the seats from the previous team. Justin slid his pad into the front pocket of the bag he'd slung over his shoulder. I adjusted my seat and turned on my headset. Everything was quiet in the ether.

"What's the big deal anyway? So I don't share your beliefs, it's never stopped us from being friends."

Justin sighed and removed his headset. "It's more than sharing the same beliefs. I believe there's an afterlife. If you accept Jesus as your savior and ask him to forgive you then he welcomes you into his presence. Heaven. If you reject him and refuse his offer of grace, then you spend eternity outside of his Presence. Hell. I don't want you to go to hell."

"Look, I see what you're saying but I can't accept that; it's too black and white. I'm not a bad person."

"Well, I am. I mess up every day. I am a bad person, but Jesus makes me better. I never used to think of myself as bad, either. I'd look around and say, I'm better than that guy, so I must be okay. But lately it's been hitting home, just how much I sin every day. The thing is, it's not the number that matters. The Bible says it only takes one sin. If you can think of only one time in your life where you did something wrong, something that hurt someone else, then you need Jesus to forgive you."

I sat there, silent, fuming even. All those years of friendship and now he was going to start lecturing me? On the other hand, this was something he cared about; these were his beliefs. What kind of friend was I if I dismissed them and ended our friendship? Then I remembered that he was only answering questions I'd asked. I'd started this; I'd opened this door. Now if only I could figure out how to close it again.

"Justin, please, this is a lot to think about. I need to process it. Don't expect me to make decision like this overnight."

"No, of course not. But lately I've felt like there isn't much time left."

"You're talking about that Rapture thing again aren't you?"

"Not really. I just don't want you to be left unprepared."

Just then a call came through, frantic and unclear, not designating who they wanted to talk to. Justin was adjusting frequencies. He paused and looked up. "Do you hear trumpets?"

My mouth was open to say no, but no sound came out. Because there was no one there to talk to.

Justin's seat was empty.

It was Judgment day, and I hadn't heard the trumpets.

I checked the frequency. The call was coming from the International Space Station. Repeating words, vanished, gone, a few expletives, and the rest broken up by sobbing. Over and over again, he would not get off the line for me to answer him nor would he say anything more coherent.

Soon I became aware of running in the hall behind me. I glanced back a couple times, wondering who else had disappeared. My best friend had vanished. Literally the one person I would process this with was gone. And he took all the answers with him.

Then I remembered. In Justin's bag was his pad, and on his pad was his Bible. I reached into his bag and pulled it out. I muted the ISS guy and began reading.

I was interrupted by the door swinging open behind me. I've heard that Earthlings think our doors slide into the wall like on old movies. But truth is hinges are much more practical.

"Mark? Where is Justin?" asked commander Harrison, our direct supervisor. She was a tall woman with constantly disheveled hair and a calm disposition.

I muted the babble coming to my station from all sources other than the ISS and opened my mouth to say he'd vanished but the words caught in my throat. "He, ah." I reached up and wiped moisture from my eyes before it could pool and run down my face.

Harrison sat across from me. "He vanished, didn't he?"

I nodded and then looked at his pad still in front of me.

"His mother is gone too. So are a lot of other people. Don't panic, Mark, we are going to find out what happened to them and hopefully get them back."

I found my voice, "It's not just here." I flipped the switch to unmute the audio from my station.

"They're gone. Everyone is gone except me. I've got some news from Earth streaming. It's the same there. Two people walking down the street and one vanishes, the camera clatters to the ground because the operator is gone, too. Yet another feed shows airplanes grounded because passengers and crew 'mysteriously vaporized.' Their words, not mine.

"I am all alone up here. I don't know why this has happened. Oh, God, space is so lonely."

Commander Harrison cut the transmission.

"Some people can't handle the unknown. You are not going to be like him, right Mark?"

"No, I won't. Because it's not unknown to me." I held up my data pad. "I might not be able to explain it very well, but I know exactly what's going on."

Commander Harrison listened. Her normally calm demeanor made it hard to tell what she thought about it. After I finished, she released me, so I could see who was left from among my friends.

I found everyone gathered in the court, a large dome set up to resemble an amphitheater. It used to be the hub of our community. It was the place to socialize and be entertained. It hadn't even been half an hour since the disappearances, and right now it was the place to connect with loved ones, trade theories, and process the impossible. Everywhere I looked, I saw people weeping. If they weren't weeping, they were staring off into space, in shock.

General Hamilton, the leader of our security operations, a glorified Sheriff really, was standing by the door watching everyone who entered. When he noticed me, I could see the relief written on his face. He was also my father. "Thank God you're alright, Mark," he said, while he gave me an embarrassing embrace.

I pulled away. How was I going to tell my strict atheist father that God was the cause of the problem? "It's good to see you too, Dad. Can I talk to you for a minute? Alone?"

"I heard about Justin, son, and I know you must have a lot of questions, but right now we need to be strong and set a calm example."

I nodded. Dad was in crisis mode. He wouldn't listen to anything I said until after the perceived danger had passed.

Commander Harrison came up behind me and said, "Sir, you may want to come to the communications room. There is an urgent call from the United Nations."

"Mom?" I asked. My mother, on returning to Earth began pursuing her old diplomatic career. She worked hard climbing the ranks, until she was the right hand of the most powerful man on the planet. If anyone would be calling from Earth right now, it would be her.

#

"Mom?" I said into the microphone and waited for her response. Technology has improved a great deal since the early days of the thirty-minute lag, but it still took about forty seconds for the signals to bounce through the void and be processed back into audible sound.

"Mark? I'm here. It's your mother. I'm sorry it's been so long since we last talked. I was so worried. I'm so glad you didn't vanish in the Culling."

"The Culling? Who's calling it a culling?" I asked.

"It's so good to hear your voice. The Culling is what we are calling it here in the UN. It's as good a name as anything, considering the kind of people who went missing."

"You mean people like Justin Orwell and his mom." I almost added *people like me*, but I was still self-conscious about numbering myself among them.

When her voice came back, it was softer, "Oh, Mark honey, I'm sorry to hear about your friend. I miss you so much, Mark. I can't wait to see you again."

"I miss you too, Mom, I can't believe you're really coming back."

"I'm not going to Mars, silly. You're coming here."

I glanced back at my dad. His face was a tight mask. The look of someone who wants to argue but knows they shouldn't. "Mom, you know why I can't come to you. I don't want to live my life from a hospital bed."

"You don't have to. The doctors have found a treatment."

"That's great, but I like it here. This is my home. Why can't you come here?"

"I couldn't even if I wanted to, dear. The UN is suspending the trade ships indefinitely. There won't be any new immigrants or imports. It's actually best if all of you left and returned to Earth. Humanity Reunited in its darkest hour."

I looked back at Dad; he was ready to talk to Mom. He said, "Say goodbye to your mother and then go wait for me at home."

I didn't go to my home. I went to Justin's.

It was a bittersweet thing. I knew I needed to say goodbye to him. But it wasn't like he died. He'd vanished, during the blink of my eye. I knew right where he was and who took him.

I pulled Justin's tablet from my bag and placed it on his bed. I'd downloaded the Bible file onto mine, so I didn't need it anymore. Also returning it felt like the right thing to do.

"God?" I looked around, still self-conscious of being over heard. "I don't know why you did this, or why you chose now to do it. But I'm feeling a little lost right now. I'm not going to ask if you're out there. I know you are. I accept the scriptures are true and that you died for me to save me from all the lies I tell. And the selfish thoughts I think."

"I really do love my mom, but I haven't seen her since I was eleven. I don't want to go. Please, show me what you want me to do. Give me a direction, and I'll follow it."

On the bed, Justin's data pad flickered to life. It was a page from the Bible. I read it and sighed. "You would have to ask me to do that, wouldn't you?"

#

The next day, Dad and the other leaders of our small government called everyone into the Court so the they could make the official announcement. At the front of the room was Dad, our Science administrator Heather Lieu, and Secretary of State Ford Fischer.

"Our community has experienced a crisis. A crisis also experienced by the population of Earth. But there it was millions of strangers, people we don't know and could never have dreamed of meeting. Here we lost friends, family, and coworkers. All vanished in the blink of an eye. Look around. The population of this colony used to fill this entire area. Now it's easy to see the damage recent events have done to our numbers. Early estimates say about forty percent of our population vanished in the crisis.

"While the nations of Earth are recovering from their own tragedies, they have given us a second crisis to handle. The UN has decided that sending ships our way would be a waste of resources. This means no more immigrants. No buyers for the metals we mine and above all, no more Brazilian coffee." Secretary Fischer paused with his lips turned upward, but his apparent joke did not receive the laugh he obviously expected.

Dad took over, "This city is not a prison but a free nation. Anyone who wants to leave is welcome to do so. But as previously mentioned we are already short-handed with no new arrivals likely. We can't really afford to lose any more manpower. But for those thinking about making a go of it on Earth, our Science Administrator has something to share."

Heather stepped forward. I felt confused to see her here since she and her family were among those who regularly attended church services.

"The UN health organization has shared a medical breakthrough that promises those who are Martian-born a normal life on Earth. All I can tell you is that it looks good on paper. I will not promise you it will work without first seeing the results of human trials. For there to be human trails, there must first be Martian-born people on Earth.

"On the subject of the vanishings, we have no scientific explanation. There were no unusual readings, no strange radiation. Those who vanished left no remains. Even their clothes went with them." Heather started tearing up. "The explanation is not scientific; it is spiritual. As most of you know, my entire family vanished. My daughter, husband, and parents were all taken. Or rather I should say, I wasn't taken with them because I learned too late that you can't fool God."

What followed was a heated debate over the pros and cons of leaving.

In the end, we left simply because we couldn't stay. Mars was nowhere near being self-sufficient. We relied on Earth for our computer chips, most of our medicine, and yes, for coffee.

#

Earth is now in sight. I am scared of spending the rest of my life in a hospital bed. But I am ready to see my mom again. I want to stand outside and try fresh air. I also want to meet people I've never met before. My world has been so small for so long. I don't know what I'll do with a whole planet to explore.

We left Mars on our own terms. But that doesn't mean we can land on Earth without being noticed. Escort ships were waiting for us at the halfway point. So much for not wasting resources. Earth knows we are here and has plans for us.

But I have faith now. Faith in Jesus Christ. He also knows we are here. And he has plans for us, too.

The End

C.O. Bonham is the pen name for a commonly misspelled first name. When she isn't writing stories of her own she is busy reading stories by others. She loves stories of all sorts but really likes the ones that are weird, or outside the norm. A homeschool graduate with a degree in creative writing, her goal is to create stories that make people think, feel, and have fun.

Visit www.cobonham.com to read author interviews, book reviews, and to hear about what she's working on next.

The Workshop at the End of the World

Kristin Janz

The workshop's bright interior felt like a sauna after the numbing midwinter cold outdoors. The old man immediately took off his fur-lined hat and gloves and started unfastening the buttons of his greatcoat. His workers glanced up from benches and forge upon his entrance, but they took too much pride in their work to set it aside and rush to greet him.

Their work was remarkable in its craftsmanship. Hand-turned wooden pull toys, sanded to a silky sheen and polished with real beeswax; stuffed animals with button and thread faces so real that he caught himself looking twice; wooden and iron puzzle games that he knew would have him scratching his own white head for hours if he attempted them. Genuine steel swords scaled down to fit an adolescent hand, some with jeweled hilts.

That last had him shaking his head. He hadn't been able to use swords as Christmas gifts in over a hundred years, and the quantity produced had always far outstripped the number of appropriate recipients. He had to trade for or purchase the toy guns he needed, because as far as the elves were concerned, gunpowder projectile weapons did not exist.

At the far end of the cavernous workshop, Lord Mitharnior stood in conference with his two cousins, all three tall, dark-haired, solemn in their agelessness. Mitharnior had led these others here long ago, refugees from a distant land that no longer knew or welcomed them. The north was cold, but they had found solace here: warm hearth fires to light the long nights, a renewed sense of purpose, meaning.

The old man grimaced. He could not allow his thoughts to travel down that path. It didn't matter how much purpose and meaning their efforts in his workshop brought the elves. Times had changed, and he could no longer afford to let them believe that they were assisting him.

Mitharnior stepped away from the others as the old man approached. "Nicholas! Well met, wizard. We have much to show you."

"Uh, yes, Mitharnior, about that..." the old man started to say, trailing off as Mitharnior strode toward the nearest workbench.

He did not have the heart to interrupt the elf lord, determined to show him each new item. He murmured admiration at gracefully strung lutes and harps (Were there any children these days who knew what a lute was, let alone how to play one?); ran a gentle finger along the snow-white fletching of handmade arrows; nodded at a tray of cooling marbles, multi-hued drops of molten glass. Inwardly, he found himself calculating how much each item could be listed for, how many hand-held gaming consoles, movie tie-in figures, and brightly-colored plastic block sets he could buy with the proceeds (the elves did not accept the existence of petroleum products, either). The numbers did not look promising.

Afterward, in an alcove off the main floor that served as Mitharnior's reception room, over steaming cups of mulled wine (the old man sipped his out of politeness only, having acquired a taste for sweeter beverages in recent years), Mitharnior asked what the problem was.

Before the old man could ask why he thought there was a problem--or insist that there wasn't--the elf said, "My question surprises you, but I can see from your countenance that you come with a heavy heart."

The old man sighed, scratching his bearded chin. "The toys, Mitharnior. The toys." He stared into the dancing flames of the small hearth, unable to meet Mitharnior's gray eyes.

"You see, I can't–They're beautiful, perfect, more than perfect. But for a long time now–"

"The children of men no longer desire such toys," Mitharnior said. "Is this what troubles you?" He set the engraved silver cup in his right hand on the low table between them. "We do not isolate ourselves as entirely as you seem to believe, Nicholas. One of my younger kinsmen–" Young to Mitharnior meant having lived fewer than a thousand years. "–went out in the world to see how the cities of men had changed. He brought back a device that I would once have called magic, a kind of seeing-eye. But I know that what used to be accomplished by magic is done now by waves of invisible light cast from tower to tower around the world."

The old man nodded. "Some children still appreciate the toys you make. Or their parents do. Other children want new, not old. I've been finding buyers for what your kinsmen and kinswomen make and using the proceeds to buy toys I can give out. But it's becoming more difficult. I'm having trouble locating enough people willing or able to pay what the items are worth. And there's the materials cost for your supplies for next year. That keeps going up. I can't afford to do this much longer, Mitharnior. I'm sorry. I should have told you before now."

Mitharnior remained silent for such a long time that the old man feared he had offended him. But when the elf spoke he said, "It is I who should be sorry. We came here to be useful and instead have become a burden to you."

"Never a burden!" the old man protested. "And you *have* been useful. I wouldn't have been able to provide gifts for so many children over the years without your help. It's just ... times have changed, and for a number of years now my pre-Christmas appearances have been more profitable than the elven handcrafts..."

"Times have changed," the elf said. "Here and elsewhere, and we find ourselves unwilling to change with them. We are not made that way. And yet, holding onto things that once were and now are not has been a cause of great evil."

The old man wanted to tell Mitharnior that he wasn't evil, far from it, but it seemed the sort of assurance offered when the speaker didn't quite believe it and so he said nothing.

He wondered if there were things he was holding onto.

Next morning the workshop was dark and silent, the elves' apartments empty. No letter or note indicated where they had gone, and the shifting drifts of snow had covered over their footprints.

But the workshop was not empty. When the old man brought a candle for light, he saw that among the handcrafted toys of wood, silk, and iron, the elves had left brand-name tablet computers indistinguishable from those fashioned in the official factories, small helicopters and cars powered by remote control, plastic dolls sporting the latest fashions and with hair in every color of the rainbow. There were toys for every child on his list, and more.

"Never a burden, Mitharnior," he murmured. "Never a burden."

The End

Kristin Janz was born in Vancouver, Canada, and since then has moved across the continent three times, ending up in the Greater Boston area for the last 20 years. Her short stories have appeared in 2 dozen different publications, including *Escape Pod*, *On Spec*, and *NewMyths.com*. "The Workshop at the End of the World" was first published in *Daily Science Fiction* in December 2015. Kristin is also a 2008 graduate of the Clarion West Writers Workshop, and the current secretary-treasurer of SF Canada, Canada's professional speculative writers' organization. She is married to fellow author Donald S. Crankshaw, with whom she

Kristin Janz co-edits and co-publishes online magazine *Mysterion*, devoted to fantasy, science fiction, and horror that engages meaningfully with Christianity, though not exclusively from a Christian perspective. *Mysterion* can be found at mysteriononline.com; Kristin's own website is at kristinjanz.com

They Stood Still

William Bontrager

Samuel Tamaki crunched down on Poky, a rod-shaped Japanese snack he engulfed during his gaming binges. It crumbled down his chin. He was crouched over in his wheelchair, eyes darting back and forth, shouting instructions to his fellow guild members. He ordered two characters with long spears to take up the rear of their party. His fingers flew over his keyboard, flesh-colored blurs, punching commands. He played angry. The only way he could. People didn't see him as a handicap in this online world of gaming. In *Quest Age*, the game that dominated his every waking hour, he was looked at as something more than just a hopeless case in a wheelchair. He was a soldier again.

Characters he fought side by side with on-screen for four hours straight now battled furiously. Goblins and Orcs were getting their heads lopped off. The soundtrack was dramatic with epic keyboard and violins. A busty magician, her name was Sindy87, conjured an ice spell and froze the attack coming from their flanks. That allowed the close attackers, two dwarves, "ChrisRoxBox13" and "i8daCheetos" to hack through the limbs of the slow-moving monstrosities -- pixelated blood and ice pellets flew. Samuel, his gamer-tag was "Sammie101," hurled poison-tipped arrows from a lethal crossbow, sniping a team of monstrous uglies from a towering ridge. One by one they fell like dirty snow. Samuel yelled instructions, sweat formed by his temple, and rage washed over him. Fake blood ran like rivers. Clashes of axes, the rush of magic spells, and shrieks of internet battles filled his senses. He was back in the battle zone, in Iraq, killing before his team got killed. He was a leader, not making mistakes, paying attention to every single detail. Life force drained from his team but he led them through the valley until the last monster was destroyed. On the mount, he put a poison tipped arrow through the eye of "DragonCaptain71." As his crew cheered, Samuel hammered his fist down on the table so hard it jostled empty Mountain Dew cans off his desk. "Air Assault!" he screamed. He took a victory swig of soda allowing the sugar-fuel to cool his boiling blood. Then he exhaled.

He finally did it! Class C. *Impossible to achieve through mere mortals!* Now he was the official leader of his group. He had been playing, *Quest Age* for three days straight, embarking on multiple small missions to become a guild commander. He had finally achieved enough experience points and had a loyal bunch of online acquaintances ready to follow him into the depths of hell if it called for that--dwarves, thieves, warriors, magicians, healers, and dark elves.

It was a day of promotion. The voices of his teammates congratulated him, but he was ready to go on. The battle ended, but the war was not over. He was gathering up the usual suspects, his battle-buddies, and preparing for the next mission. The outside world had nothing to offer, and he'd sleep when he was dead.

He was about to hit the "Save" button when suddenly his monitor froze.

What! For any gamer of Samuel's caliber, this was more than an inconvenience. He shook his head in disbelief.

"Nuu-ooh! Not now."

Samuel tapped on his headset. *Nothing.* He pinched the connectors. Same story. He looked frantically around. No one on the screen moved an inch except his own character. His dark robed figure impatiently paced near a fountain. His busty ice magician teammate held an erotic pose in her skimpy armor but she never swayed from that spot. He wriggled his mouse pad back and forth, punched some keys, and waited, but they all stood like statues.

The game's save point could not be reached, either, because "Sammie101" had attached himself to the guild already. That meant if they didn't move to a different location, he couldn't move either. This was one of the coolest and most realistic features of the game usually -- the complete dependence on each other as you went on quests. It was this social element that enticed Samuel to become a hermit for months on end, barely showering, living on noodles and take out, never doing laundry. All of these things were evident even taking a cursory glance around his tiny, stale apartment.

The "social" element of the game screwed him this time. The save point was just down the cobbled path, out of reach and glowing. He tried to disband from his group but the controls prevented him from advancing; he couldn't even switch his weapons. *Raggh!*

And if he re-set the game, he would lose his rank and would have to repeat the last six quests. That also meant the great online team he amassed might be off doing some other missions when he logged back on. It was only the luck of the draw that none of his current team members were bratty thirteen-year-olds.

"Can anyone hear me? Mayday! Ground control to Major Tom," he said into his mic, but he received no response back.

His dark elf character, clad in silver armor, black greaves, and black cloak, darted around the group. Just like Samuel, his character appeared puzzled. He tested the microphone again. Useless. The symphonic soundtrack of the game was on full blast seconds before the freeze. Now there was only the seashell chorus from the noise dampening headphones suction cupped to his ears.

"No, no, no, no!" Samuel croaked.

He cursed again. He was hyped to go on his leadership mission. Now it would have to wait as he scrambled to troubleshoot his equipment. After minutes of sweating and cursing he had to admit defeat. Seeing no other option, he reluctantly pushed the switch to re-boot the computer. Four hours down the drain. But he would get it back.

This was his destiny!

But when it came back on again, he was back in the same place, game still frozen, same magician in the same erotic pose. Same two dwarves faced each other with red grimaces and heavy axes. Above their spiked helms the names "ChrisRoxBox13" and "i8daCheetos" were parallel and un-moving as billboards.

"No! This can't be happening," screeched Samuel.

He banged his fists on the arm of his wheelchair. *Why, Gaming Gods!* His mind raced. It had to be a problem on the company's end! He wheeled around sharply and spilled a half a cup of noodles on his hard wood floor. He searched for his phone. He knew the technical hotline to the game by heart now. He'd call and find out what the deal was.

As he rolled forward, his progress was halted by a stray sock that got caught up in his wheel. He had no time to play around. This was "*Quest Age*," after all. He reversed his wheel chair and maneuvered around it in a huff. His phone was buried somewhere under all the garbage on the coffee table. It was glass but you couldn't see that by all the discarded pizza boxes, empty Chinese takeout containers, paper plates and Mountain Dew cans that made up the face of it. It looked more like a lump of garbage on four wooden legs -- a modern art exhibit sprouted by intense periods of isolation.

He fished his phone from under a few paper plates with pizza residue. He tried to dial the number but his phone, like the game, was also frozen. The thought of getting back to the game was like a fever. It wasn't just that he enjoyed the quests…it was his life now.

#

Samuel was just a rail thin kid, half-Hawaiian half-Asian, that fit the stereotype of a typical gamer -- too many pimples, average looks, and a quiet, awkward demeanor. His father was a lifelong soldier, and after graduating high school, Samuel followed his Sergeant Major Daddy down a similar path. He started as a mechanic, and as good as he was in video games and critiquing Anime, he was better at dissembling an M-4 while remaining lake-calm under extremely volatile battle conditions.

When he was stationed in Camp Speicher near Tikrit, he had plans of reenlisting as an 11 Bravo Infantry, then maybe work his way to Ranger. He wanted to be just like Dad, Army ranger for the Big Red One. But the improvised explosive device, a.k.a. roadside bomb, that attacked his convoy heading from Tikrit to Mosul was merciless and sudden. Like the Humvee, the explosion flipped his world upside down. In a flash of blood, shrieks, and pain, he awoke in Landstuhl, Germany, in a warm hospital, not a cold fold-up cot in the desert. His legs were torn to the bone by shrapnel. He had to be cut down from the knees down. Then he was flown back home to Nevada, his purpose shattered.

The video games he engulfed himself in proved better therapy than the sessions with the psychologist and the anti-depressants. She handed them out like they were Pez.

Three years went by like a haze in the world of gaming. Samuel played *Battle Realm*, then *R.E.T.U.R.N. Force*, then went through his anime collections and when that got old he found more games to get lost in. No real interaction with real people. Fantasy was much easier. In Fantasy, nobody really died. The guilt did not last. He felt that the world outside did not see him at all. Especially growing up in Las Vegas, where everything moved in a superficial blur.

#

"Of all the days this could happen!" Samuel yelled.

He banged his fist on the armrest. He wiped a line of sweat from his forehead. The air conditioner unit that normally sputtered out a thin trail of moldy water was silent. He rolled past the couch to his door. Surely his neighbors had a phone he could use. He rapped three times, but he couldn't hear anything on the other side…nothing at all.

"DeMeka. Hey. This is Sam. I was wondering if I could use your phone?"

No response. Weird. He knocked on the remaining four doors down the hallway. The same eerie silence met him. He lived in a poor neighborhood in downtown. The odds of none of his unemployed neighbor's being home were extremely slim.

"Where's everybody?"

He headed towards the entrance, down the ramp to the paint-chipped back door. He was in such a frenzy of emotion that he wasn't aware he passed a single leaf, frozen, in mid-air, dangling below the window. The leaf floated there like magic. He didn't notice the particles of individual dust pellets that hung in the air either. He didn't notice his landlord holding a sandwich in the corner. His eyes closed, his mustache brushed the bread, face locked in a grimace, dull eyes stared ahead.

Samuel Tamaki didn't realize his world stood still until he rolled out on the street. Then he couldn't help but notice.

#

What the!

Samuel's city was frozen, shut down. A world locked down from time. Cars, people, things, were in the position of motion *minus* the motion. The world was stark still–like his game upstairs and his phone in his pocket. People were mannequins. Birds were petrified, stiff wings, as if they were suspended on invisible cables.

The light that said **WALK**, never flashed to **DON'T WALK**. Cars were movie props with no engines.

But Samuel saw enough practical jokes on YouTube that he didn't show his surprise. He remembered a particular video of a huge host of people that did the same thing in a mall when some famous celebrity left a store.

That's what it is. A joke.

It's gotta be. The people in the video were ordered at a certain time to stand completely still. It was a ruse, an adult version of "Red Light, Green Light" where the red light was always on.

He wheeled down the sidewalk with a grin, despite the strange bubbling feeling stirring in his gut. He laughed into the soundless street. Further down, there were more stiff people.

These actors are really good.

They must have used props too. He glided further down. Nobody budged yet. A tall man with a newspaper under his arm looked like he was guarding Buckingham palace, his body locked into an absurd paralysis.

Samuel crossed to the other side of the street. There had to be some people who weren't in on the joke.

The back of the taxi's suspended exhaust smoke must be some plastic molding or some kind of trick with a mirror or something. He went further down the block, mouth agape.

This giant performance can't be for me. There must be some big celebrity in town. He laughed but he didn't like the sound of his voice. How hollow it was.

The street stretched out. That gnawing feeling in his gut grew worse. His breakfast tried to surge past his throat. Dry lips too. *Like that time… No! Just stop. Assess. Alright?* If the whole block was playing a trick he didn't want to be the one dumb guy that gave it away. *It's best to just keep silent…*And he would watch. He stayed still for several minutes, careful to look around with his peripherals, on the lookout for any movement. He marveled about how real it all looked. So far not a single child scampered out with a book bag, not a single car beeped impatiently for people to move.

Just how far down does it go?

Minutes ticked by or so he assumed, since his phone was stuck. The people were still as ever. Nobody shifted their weight, scratched their nose, sneezed, or curled a lip. Was the whole block closed off for this? *This is Vegas. Impossible to pull off.* He needed to get a closer look.

He saw a woman nearby who was checking her cell phone before she decided to absurdly pause. She was a banker type – power suit, powder blue, black hose, big purse, heavy eye shadow. She didn't blink once. He wheeled to her carefully. The way her body was positioned, it would take an incredible feat of strength to hold a pose like that, a yoga master. *Or a fake. So get a grip.* She was stepping off the sidewalk; or rather she still was in the process of stepping off. By the way she was balanced, on the tip of her toes, just a brush, or a slight breeze would throw her balance off. But she didn't move a muscle.

Because she's fake, man!

It was an easy explanation.

Samuel wheeled closer to the woman, palms sweating. He reached out to try to get her to break character a little, at least enough to assure him.

He nudged her. In air, she fell, tipping to the ground, her arm was still crooked. Her head remained bent towards her cell phone. She fell over like any mannequin would.

She fell on the street just like that, in that same position. But he heard a sound he didn't expect. Something cracked... faint, but unmistakable. A wet thud. It made his skin dance. The woman laid there, mute, eyes open, face bent up to his in the same vacant stare, lips slightly parted, completely still. Then blood leaked down over her ears and pooled beside his chair.

All of his defenses suddenly crumbled. The "fake" had a real skull, and it just smacked on the concrete like a cantaloupe. *Oh, God!* He lurched over, dug his nails in the arms of his wheelchair. Not again! He looked down as the woman's eyes were shimmering glass. She seemed to be silently pleading for help. Yet he could not. Not this time. Not last time either.

"No! No! I didn't do anything. Someone help her!"

He looked around. But nobody ran to her aide.

He banged his chair with both fists, face reddening. The girl was not his responsibility. He didn't do anything wrong.

"It's not my fault!"

Spittle flew in ropes out of his mouth.

He let out a roar that echoed down the block.

"It's not my fault! "

No help came. The blood pool expanded around where Samuel's feet may have been.

Samuel's mind turned over and over. The sterile air suffocated him; the mute faces stared ahead. The woman looked up at him like she was already lying in her casket.

No! She is dying. Pick her up.

No. She's a dummy. Strawberry brains. Movie props!

Save her!

Damn! He wheeled closer to her and grabbed her hair, squeezed his eyes, and with all his strength, he righted her limp form to a sitting position against a tire well. He swallowed down his anger seeing the woman's head loll sideways like a doll. This was not fair. He was fine in Quest Age. He injured nobody. Now this! Now…Stop!

"This!" he screamed up at the sky, veins jutting out of his neck.

But she was heavy. Far more than a crash test dummy. She laid back on the ground, mouth parted almost sensuously.

Get away, Sammie!

Salty tears tickled around his eyes.

Go!

He pedaled away from his familiar street, away from the woman. He wheeled as fast as he could, glancing from side to side hoping to find some movement, a helping hand. Heck. Even an ant crawling over a crack would ease his mind. Down the block was the same. Tourists poised to snap pictures, people slumped against the wall; people crossed the street, people leaned out of taxis; people looked out of the windows of little coffee shops. None of them stirred.

Props, Sam. Props. Then what happened to the weather? Forget that. Move. *Hup!*

Further down, faster. There had to be some kind of explanation.

But where was the heatwave?

I'm in Nuke Town, plastic re-configured map in the game Call of Duty. I'm in a video game. Crazy. But this air? It's like electric. There was no wind. *No. Not Nuke Town, man. That world's shiny and new.*

This place is Vegas, as old as sin itself.

Sin.

He wheeled past the crumbling infrastructure. The roads were peppered with orange cones and construction signs. Where North Las Vegas Boulevard met South, he crossed. The streets were narrow here. He took the right lane, looking into the cars. Faces stared ahead expecting traffic to move. One man, dwarf-looking, had a liver spotted hand to his horn. Near Freemont Street, he passed a graffiti wall of an alien trapped in its yellow and white bricked prison. He passed the gaudy pink Bail Bonds building with its painted red lips, the Graceland Wedding Chapel; EZ Pawn and Jewelry, and thousands of more people, thousands of eyes. But no one helped.

This is a nightmare. *No. Must be a reason. Have I been drugged? Maybe bad Dew.*

Ha-ha- get real Sam. What else? Cough medicine? War flashback? *Oh God, please…not that.*

That woman. The puddle of blood. That hideous, fluid weight when I dragged her.

She looked like a female soldier he remembered from his unit. Her body was crushed in between a jack-knifing trailer two days after getting to his duty station. He couldn't help her either. It happened too swiftly; like everything in war. If he was going insane there would be no battle-buddy to see him through this time, no one to pull him out of the rubble.

He travelled down the air-less street. The sun stood still. He didn't hunger, thirst; that worried him more than the weather. He hadn't tired even though he had wheeled for miles. In some places, he had to force himself uphill. Physically, he was impervious. He bit his lip hard -- blood ran freely down his chin, but he didn't feel it at all, no outside stimuli.

But his mind was in constant pain, haunted by memories of the past. He felt the hideous laughter of a world with no stimuli. His mind stored time, touched it, needed social interaction, and thrived on stimulus. None of these were granted to him.

This is why inmates go crazy under isolation.

He once read about an experiment done where monkeys were put in a huge pit with plastic slippery sides. They frantically struggled for minutes to climb out before giving up in despair. They spent the rest of the time hunched over, hope lost. Suicidal creatures.

"*I'm* not an animal."

He was jolted by the sound of his voice.

He crossed the congestion of cars on Carson Avenue. Out a car window, a hand tossed a cigarette that never made it to the ground. After a few miles the street opened up to the major casinos and hotels. The palm trees got bigger and gaudier the further south he travelled. They pointed the gamblers and high-rollers in the right direction, like shaggy creatures out of a Dr. Seuss book. When the road widened further, the world got even weirder. Stretch limos, white security vehicles; women with noses high in the air, girls images advertising on billboards and buses; signs over them, 1-900 numbers, all scattered along the strip like a kid clumsy with his Lego's. To his right, people were packed in the George Wallace restaurant (a grinning, taunting, George Wallace sign above the awning). To the left, The Flamingo loomed. Inside restaurants, people had their glasses raised, or had barbecue sauce on their lips, or were smirking, eyes wide and haunting, or caught in mid-laugh, oblivious to their environment. Further on, he passed Caesar's Palace now. He gripped his wheels, rolling faster passing all of the faces. Hoped he wasn't going mad. Fearing he already had.

That was when the voice started whispering to him. It scared him to the core.

"*No answer.*" It mocked.

Stop it soldier. Get a grip. This is a hallucination. Caused by…what?

"*War.*" It hissed.

Samuel shook his head. That was just panic. That isn't what a soldier is made of.

"*Sammie.*" It whispered.

Stop. *That's not my name!* Keep wheeling. Keep on trucking. Get through this. You got this, you…

"Can't."

"*Sammie.*" The voice said.

That voice sounded like Samuel's except it was empty of all hope, stressed out, lost, alone and hoarse, perhaps from screaming at people online. It was a voice of no-hope.

#

Samuel gazed at the painted signs of all the casinos surrounding him, crowding him. He couldn't roll fast enough past them, like his wheels were stuck in wet cement. He could no longer take the blank stares. He wheeled around. Panic creeped slowly through his arteries, pumping ice into his heart. That lone voice followed him. Then his eyes widened at the plastic world around him.

I was wrong. This world wasn't empty at all.

I'm being watched.

It was full of enemies.

They started to mutter. Their faces like stone, their mouths never moved. But he heard them all. Laughing, toasting, plotting. They whirled all around him, threatening.

"*He's the one.*"

"Kill the soldier." They whispered.

He spun his chair around, but nobody visible advanced. The enemy hid behind the shells. Just like they did back then.

Back then…

Keep moving soldier. Move.

He forced himself to push his chair through enemy lines. Sliding under the pillars of a Roman-style bridge, their voices got stronger. They came from all around him, even from above, in the windows of the hotels, over Corinthian style pillars and marble ledges. The sounds of monsters, depraved humans, white noise. He wheeled faster, arms pumping, hands burning on the rubber of his wheels. Needed to get away. But the convoy…

He heard that other cruel voice.

"You are alone."

"You can never leave…"

"Alone."

"Behind enemy lines"

"No!"

He's was in the middle of the street, near the Luxor when he hit a wide crack in the street. It threw him to the ground, and the voices shouted like a war cry. They were crawling all over him, taking advantage of his downed form.

"Help! Please! Help meeeeee…." He babbled, before…

The pent up emotion, the panic, the agony of not knowing when the enemy would strike, the feeling of being all alone, eked out of him in a groan. He clawed at the air, writhing on the ground, rolling into the cracked surface of the concrete. Waiting for death. Waiting for the mortar, or the round, or…The voices accused him. He low-crawled away, dragging his stubs and elbows along the ground.

"You'll never move fast enough, Sammie."

"Never."

"Game over."

"Please," he babbled.

Then he heard a distant rumbling. He glanced up. *No! No! No!* But there it was. There was the chipped paint of the olive grill cage appearing through a red mist. There was the familiar roar of the engine, the lurch of the Allison transmission. The soldiers were inside. One had a camcorder out, recording a mocking moment of cadence-singing, hearkening back to those days when they were forced to sing. Laughter mingled with chants.

"No. Not this."

"*One -oh -One*," they sang.

"*Patch on mah - shoulder*"

The Humvee was twenty feet from him. He crawled on his hands and knees, shouting for them to stop, but the dust was so thick he had to keep his head ducked. Then he felt the fur on his fingers, glanced up into the red-orange haze.

"No. No! NO!" Samuel croaked.

Black watery eyes glared back at him, judging him. The Eyes of the dog. The one he didn't see all those years ago. His hand was on the matted fur, caked with blood. He pulled it away. "Please. Not like this." The creature's open, bloody mouth was locked into a stretched out, ghastly expression of laughter.

"*Yes. Exactly like this.*" That voice seemed to say.

The Humvee was so close he could feel the heat of the engine.

"No! Don't!" Samuel shouted blind from swirling dusts and sudden heat. Until then the fear was tamped down. But the seismic rotations inside of him matched the rumble of the approaching vehicle.

Too late. He was re-living it all. The bomb, the Humvee, the convoy. He put up his hands. The tires closed in. He screamed, lungs filled up with ash, mouth overextended, eyes wide and white, laced with terror.

The soldiers were oblivious as they sang. He heard the roar and then blackness like the vehicle had gone over him. For a moment he thought he, and they, were safe. The vehicle seemed to pass by and there was a moment of calm, and then…

His world exploded in fire and death. He felt drawn in the flame and darkness, sucked through its merciless vacuum. His arms, legs, his face, his feet, kicked, in flames, screaming, screaming, hearing the death-cries of his crew…drawn into the flames where the tears he cried boiled...spasms rippled through his helpless frame like he was being shocked again and again. The flashbacks of war poured over him. The images berated him in the middle of the soundless street.

War.

The explosion killed everyone else.

Why did I make it?

#

He heard nothing but the ringing in his ears and the tortured cries of that fateful day. The tears had poured down and mingled in the dust; the great heavy sobs made his whole body shudder.

He repeated over and over:

Why me?

#

For how long he remained there, nobody but God knew because time here was an illusion. He was in a black-out state, on the ground motionless, curled up in the fetal position. His eyes wide open.

His phone went off.

"*Get up, Samuel.*"

The sound of the phone had toyed with his ears. In a world of no stimuli, it was enough to stir him. Like butterfly wings, his lids opened with many attempts. His grimaced in agony and gingerly, feeling every bone and nerve on fire, he crawled to his upturned wheelchair. The cell was lighting up beside it; it piped a programmed jingle. He crawled, out of breath and reached for the phone. He needed this. Somebody needed to be on the other end. Somebody needed to make sense of this. But he saw it was just an alarm he had set back when things were normal. He tried to push other buttons, try to call out, get some help, but no other function worked. How the phone even worked in that capacity was a mystery. He kept it in his hand, listening to the alarm-music before it finally cut out.

Silence.

Now what? Why'd he wake up?

Why didn't the world just let him die?

Now what?

Then he heard another voice, commanding, firm, yet controlled.

"You have to move, Son."

"The enemy is here."

He did. Now righted, he continued south, shoulders hunched, eyes staring straight ahead, resembling the mute people all around him.

That commanding voice had vanished though. What replaced it was the mocking one, the sad one. The one that called him only by his gaming tag.

"Sammie, there is only one solution to your problem."

He was tired of fighting the voice.

"One answer." Samuel repeated it.

He made an involuntary left at Tropicana, a long stretch of highway. After miles of passing places like Hooters Hotel and desolate looking strip malls, he was in the suburbs. There were few cars here, hardly any people outside. Nothing left. It was like everybody was holed up awaiting a giant storm. He made his way down the middle of the road, automatically, slowly, looking for a way to escape. Heeding that one lone voice.

"Sammie, Death is the only escape – the only solution."

Samuel nodded. The way to do it was to shatter a window, cut the life-cord hidden under the wrist with a shard. He glanced at the row of houses to either side of him. Shatter a window? He doubted he even had the strength to do that.

"What's that over there?" Samuel asked himself.

"That's the end of the line, Sammie boy. Ha– quite literally."

He wheeled to it.

Until then, everything else in his environment stubbornly resisted his requests. When Samuel cried for help, he was looked on by soulless eyes. When he shrieked for sympathy or mercy, he was transported back to the war to relive his nightmare instead. But now that he wished for death, this world gladly accommodated him.

"End of the line." Samuel said.

Three feet from him, hanging from a lamp post, tailor made for him, was a noose. Just the right height for someone confined to a wheelchair. All he would have to do is slip his head under it and kick out his wheelchair. As smooth as a duck along a pond. He wheeled to the rope.

"One solution."

He slipped the rope over him, and that raspy voice chuckled in his head.

"Now kick out, Sammie. End it all. End us. End our misery. Let's join our dead mother." The voice hissed.

My mother?

His mother died from cancer while he was recovering. He lost his best friend in life, the only woman who ever saw anything in him.

Mother. His legs were stumps, but all he did was grin, joke, pretend it didn't affect him, pretend it was alright, and got lost in the shimmer of his computer screen- a world he could control. Staying in Vegas, turning away any help from good friends. He didn't seek it – he didn't need it. The nightmares hit, and he shrugged off the symptoms of a war-syndrome, and stayed true, stayed strong. *Like Dad.*

Or so he had thought.

"There is no one left, Sammie."

He had to agree. He tightened the noose around his neck.

Ready.

Hot tears coursed down his cheeks. Regrets. When people were around, he shunned them. The thought repeated in his mind. Alone. Orphan. Pathetic. Moaning now, a hideous sound like an ancient ceremonial horn, his tears rained down his neck, his body trembling, suddenly going cold.

I've made a mess of things. I've forsaken real life for a fake one. Now I'm seeing what it was truly like to be alone, to be hurting, in a world that can't react. I brought this on myself.

This is what I deserve.

There were no tears left. What was shock early on, had become fear, then regret but now it morphed into a heavy depression, narrated by that hideous voice inside Samuel's head.

"Do it then, Sammie!" it said.

But Samuel still halted. He had some things still left.

He still had his mother.

Her beautiful smile appeared in his mind.

He still had the voice of his father. And he could hear him. That was who told him the enemy was there earlier. It was there now, too.

"Soldier on. Soldiers fight, Son." He said.

My father? What would he think about his son right now? A noose around his neck? Yes, his sweet mother is gone but his father was still alive. He was serving his country with honor somewhere. Samuel hesitated, his chair slanted up to the sky. Just another push and he can end the misery. But that voice of his father wrestled with that raspy voice.

"*Soldiers die,*" The other voice reminded him.

"Yes. We die," Samuel said.

You can't argue with that logic. Look at his friends. Dead in mere seconds. And Dad? He left him and his mother early on. So what did he know about soldiering? Where was he when the biopsy came back positive? No, Dad couldn't help him now. Once the chair slips away he would be in the air, hanging; it will be over. He didn't know how it would feel, but it was nothing compared to being here, being trapped. Samuel leaned further back, wheels to the grey sky, tears bubbling down his lips, cheeks trembling, chest pounding.

"Push it!" The raspy voice sang out.

He still hesitated. Fighting out of the fog of the trauma in his mind was another memory and then a realization, of his surroundings.

He was on Spencer Street. His home.

"Hey!"

"I'm on Spencer Street!" Samuel croaked.

"Who cares? What are you doing?"

He exhaled that poison air and he levelled out his wheelchair, wheels smacking against the concrete, jarring the chair even as the angry, ugly voice roared its disapproval.

This is where I grew up.

Spencer Street was in an era before everything changed.

Is it still there?

"Turn and find out, Son." Dad's advice.

He turned his head, still in the noose. Yes. There it was. Still there. Wow! It didn't change. Hotels came and went but it hasn't. The same church he went to as a little boy. It was where he was baptized as a child, swimming through a tub of tepid water, barely able to understand what "baptism" meant.

The noose scratched his neck. But the cruel voice persisted.

"Do I have to remind you? This is where it all began. Your dad leaves you. This is the street where your mom got cancer. Don't get sentimental. We have a job to do. Let's get to it, Sammie!"

But Samuel never thought of Spencer Street like that.

It represented what?

Possibility.

"Yes. Possibility." Samuel whispered. "And family."

Hope, too.

Slowly he removed the noose from his head, pushing the weight off of him. The horrible voice, that gruff thing, roared, but it was like one now falling from a long distance. Not as something in control anymore. Besides, he knew where the rope hung, and he could always go back. But maybe there would be a reason not to.

#

The door of the little church was open. They also had a wheelchair ramp for him, accommodating him like the noose had seconds earlier. That's as rational a reason as any to further explore.

Inside, a man waited for him. Samuel saw it through a hazy, numb fog. The various stages he had just experienced were a storm that sapped him of much strength.

"Are you real?" Samuel said.

Samuel waved limply.

The man sat on the back row pew and craned his head. His hands were in his lap with his legs crossed. He was reading a hymnal. When he smiled, his honey eyes lit up. A dimple formed on one cheek. "Hello, Samuel. You've been through a lot. You can rest now. No more rolling," he said closing the book.

Possibility.

Samuel nodded, unable to grasp if he was hallucinating.

The man gestured. "Here, let me help." He wheeled Samuel to the front of the altar where he sat on the front pew to face him. His suit swished with the slightest movement.

"I would have met you sooner, but I hate being so close to these casinos. Such…fake stuff. I like genuine things. Y'know, what I mean Samuel? Besides, you needed that long depressing last stretch so you'd be receptive to what I am about to say. Not that we did this, but management allowed it," the man said with tenderness.

Samuel's soundless trek made his ears extra sensitive to stimuli. Being deprived of those senses for so long, he welcomed each syllable out of the stranger's mouth like every hypnotic note from "Ave Maria." The man grinned, showing slightly crooked teeth.

Other than that, he was soap-opera handsome.

"You guessed it yourself. It isn't rocket science. You are here because you neglected society," The man said. "All these special creations and you opted for what? Pixels?"

He cleared his throat.

Samuel looked up at the beautiful stained glass windows in a daze. His eyes followed the colors.

"How did I get here?" Samuel asked.

"This church."

"No. Here. All around?"

The man smoothed his tie. "You were put in the hole, Samuel. Isolation. Like how they have in prison."

Samuel smirked. "Like the monkeys?"

"You're much more than that, but yes, in a way. You see, as soon as your personal computer glitched, you, like the dust that you were made from, were plucked out of your own time-line."

"How'd that happen?"

The man checked his watch.

"We call it an 'out-of-time' experience," the man said.

Samuel nodded. "Out of time--but how?"

"A cataclysmic event, similar to a storm blacking out a neighborhood," the man said.

"And it shut down time? It made everything stand still? Can you manipulate time?" Samuel asked.

"*We* can't," the man said. "We're just given certain instructions."

The man rose up and walked to the front, pointing to the many-colored patterns of the stained glass windows where Samuel's eyes were focused.

"I understand this is all confusing for you, Samuel."

Samuel nodded again. Light, colors, and vibrations were emanating from beyond the stained glass window. The stranger's fingers sent out trails. Golden light swirled around Samuel. It felt warm on his skin.

"What is this?" Samuel said referring to the light and sensations. Light seemed to be moving on its own like butterflies all around the church.

The suit-and-tie fellow nodded.

"There are realms within realms Samuel. Your frozen world here is sort of a gateway into another place, and that can be a door to another one. How do you think I got here?" he said.

Sammie marveled at the vibrations swirling around the church.

"So, in one great big event I was expelled from my own timeline," Samuel said.

The mystery man leaned on the pulpit.

"It happened in less than a second. It is very layered and a little over-my-head. The guys over in engineering could explain it better." The man laughed.

Samuel thought about his old drill sergeant.

"Layered. We were taught a cadence in Basic training like that? There's a hole in a hole, and a log in the hole and a frog in the hole," Samuel said.

"I guess it's a little like that," the man said and grinned.

Samuel smiled, looking up at the colors dancing behind the stained glass.

What color is that?

Is it new?

He rolled closer to the light. He wanted to go into it further, to melt into that beyond. But the man stopped him.

"Don't get too close to these doorways, Samuel," he said, and when he did the lights flickered in the church. There was a faint rumble.

The man grimaced.

"I'm afraid we need to cut this short."

The man leapt off the carpeted platform. Samuel couldn't stop staring now as the windows seemed to be melting, pouring out radiant light, drawing him toward it like a vacuum.

The swirling patterns!

Oh! Oh My!

A slow smile formed around Samuel's mouth that spread wider as he tried to catch a glimpse of the radiant swirling mass of light. He couldn't. The man was behind him now, wheeling him to the very front of the church, talking hastily.

"I'm glad we could talk. I'm glad you didn't listen to that other voice. You listened to him for so long before. But you proved you *are* a soldier. You fought through this mess and made it all the way back to me. You overcame the noose temptation. You know what that tells me, Samuel?"

"No. What?"

The man leaned over and whispered in his ear and grabbed his frozen cell phone as the church walls quivered.

"It tells me you want to live," he said.

The man hit a few buttons on Samuel's phone. It suddenly came to life.

Destination: Three miles away.
"Turn Right at Spencer Street."

"Three miles left, Samuel. Do you have it in you?" the man said.

Samuel took the phone, saw the blinking arrow and nodded slowly. No more questions. Finally, he had direction in the madness. Before Samuel could turn around and thank the stranger, the man was gone. The church was tiny, and the wide road was before Samuel. Samuel could feel rumblings in the sky. He knew it was urgent he get to where the GPS directed him and quickly. He wanted to live. He pumped his arms as fast as they could go.

#

The GPS led him to Sunrise hospital. Like everything there, ambulances were paused in motion. Down the hallways, still guided by the GPS, he saw nurses carrying measurements of medication, patients leaning out of their rooms mannequin-stiff and doctors looking serious, carrying clipboards. He glided through the open double doors marked *Emergency* and wheeled down the hallway. The phone indicated he was at his destination. He glanced ahead. Down the hall bathed in shadows he saw a soldier in digital camouflage leaning over somebody in a bed on wheels. There was a nurse beside the soldier, hands out as if she was explaining something to him before time froze. Samuel got closer, feeling something stirring in his veins. He recognized the man somehow. The football-broad shoulders, the salt and pepper hair, the slant in the eye from the side angle. And then closer yet, Samuel saw clearly who it was and all the breath left his lungs. He gasped, eyes bright and widening. "Dad!" He drew closer yet and his hands stuck on his wheels. He looked again. It was no mistake. He cried out in the noiseless hall. His father, in full uniform right down to the laced-up desert boots, looked down at the figure in the bed. The man's coarse hand brushed the top of the pillow where matted hair was.

Samuel wheeled around, mouth moving but saying nothing. There was care in his father's eyes and a tear frozen over his cheek. *Dad!* Samuel saw his father's love frozen in that moment. It overwhelmed his heart.

Then he looked down. He saw his own frail form in that bed, another Samuel. This Samuel had a bandage over his skull, breathing-tube snaked around and through his nose. This

Samuel was the one his father was crying over. He saw himself, head resting on the pillow, eyes closed.

What happened to me? The man in the church told him something had happened that he couldn't say. This was it.

This is what being in isolation prepared me to go through.

Samuel balled his hands into fists.

Alright. Let's go.

Samuel saw a brilliant glare, felt his body go light, felt himself rise from the wheelchair and before that transition from the wheelchair to the bed, he heard voices, movement, instructions, sneakers on the floor, time returning, his father sobbing, the nurse telling Command Sergeant Major Tamaki that his son had suffered from a brain aneurism. It ruptured. Emergency surgery was undertaken. She told him that Samuel was lucky that they got to him right away.

Your personal computer glitched.

Somewhere in that void, Samuel smiled thinking about the man's words.

"A cataclysmic event." It will be the hardest thing he'll ever face.

They Stood Still

But there are people who love me.

They want to help me.

My Dad is here now.

And when Samuel recovers and has the option to turn on "*Quest Age*," instead he'll go out and explore Las Vegas.

I choose real life.

And I'll start with the church I grew up in.

Before Samuel's eyes fluttered open, he thought back to when he was just little and Dad laid on his back and played airplane with him, feet up on Samuel's stomach, holding him in the air, and how the wind blew through little Samuel's hair, and Dad laughed until his face got red, and they collapsed in a heap, father and son. Now there was a possibility to redeem that magical time.

Despite time returning, tears of joy were frozen on Samuel's cheeks.

The End

William Bontrager served as a mechanic in Operation Iraqi Freedom from 05-06 as a Screaming Eagle in the 101 Air Assault Division. His key inspirations to write are Spider-Man comics and Stephen King novels, and he aims to entertain with his stories while also speaking truth.

He's a long-time fan of science fiction and has written numerous unpublished short stories. He's also a visual artist who has a gallery of his works available online at:

They Stood Still
https://williambontragerportfolio.weebly.com/

The Memory Dance

A.K. Meek

For two minutes of Sullivan's perilous journey down the mountain pass, Providence kept him on the road that had suddenly fallen away under a blizzard of sheep-sized snowflakes and northern white-out.

In minute three, Providence turned its watchful eye to the nearby woods.

Sullivan turned his SUV left while the roadway veered right, and the guardrail did nothing more than shriek in tin-can fury as his vehicle tore through and dove into a shallow revetment. His Japanese manufacture SUV didn't stand a chance against a 200-year-old slowly dying oak.

Airbags violently deployed in a pre-packaged factory explosion.

The SUV came to a crunching halt, spraying ethylene glycol life fluid, the wrenching crash spooking nesting woodpeckers in a hollow portion of the tree trunk. Flaps carried them away into the unfit winter storm.

After a minute, a thin cry shook Sullivan from his post-crash fugue state. He had the most horrible dream that he had run off the road and tumbled down a cliff. Before he slammed to the bottom, in which he would surely die, he awoke.

Realizing his dream wasn't far from true, he grasped wildly at the passenger seat, before his eyes could register sight. "Felly," he cried out in emotionally charged panic. His mind shot away to how Patricia would react to this. He had his daughter one weekend a month and nearly killed her during that time. "Felly!" he called again. Patricia would never let him hear the end of it.

"Da," came Felicity's reply, choked with her father's fear and ten-year-old incomprehension of what just happened.

Sullivan let out a laugh-cry as his hand stumbled towards her voice. Immediately his fingers wandered over her cheek and head and neck with the grim task of searching for lacerations or gaping wounds. "My baby, are you okay?"

"Da," she repeated, her voice stronger than before.

He pushed away the airbag that was slowly losing air and reached for the Life-Sav auto response button mounted on his rearview mirror. It should've activated with the collision but hadn't.

He pressed the button. "Hello," he shouted, his voice tenor from adrenaline. "We were in an accident and need help!" His words froze in small puffs of fog as the warm SUV interior was overcome by cold. Involuntarily he shivered, a little from the cold, a lot from the situation he now faced.

A long minute and there was no response from anything.

He released his seatbelt and stretched to unbuckle his daughter, still partially enveloped in the collapsed airbag.

Fortunately, his door opened with little resistance and he guided his daughter out of the mangled vehicle and stood her upright. As soon as he gained his feet a shockwave of pain rippled up his left leg. The cold air blasted his face. "We need to bundle up." These words also froze on the air.

The blizzard that had been raging for the past couple of days had slightly tapered in intensity. Now, the moment was illuminated in that odd time when you couldn't tell if it was supposed to be daytime or nighttime. What little light remained reflected off white blankets and gave the impression of an early, winter morning even though you knew it was all deceptive, at best.

Sullivan rushed to the back of his ruined SUV that had been his pride and joy for the past two months. He forced the hatch open. He tossed running shoes and baseball mitts aside searching for a couple of thin blankets he kept back here, just in case. This event was one of those *just in case* moments if there ever was one.

"Put this on, Felly." He draped one blanket over his daughter's shoulder, over her jacket. "Are you warm? Are you alright?"

She nodded and wiped stray strands of golden hair from her face. Hair like her mother's.

He needed to let his wife know, to let someone know. After throwing the other blanket over himself, he pulled his cell phone from his pocket and made two attempts to dial with quickly-numbing fingertips. His phone showed no available network. He kept his swearing inside so his daughter wouldn't hear. Instead, he slammed his SUV hatch closed with more force than necessary, shattering the glass.

They needed to find shelter. But last he remembered, they were in between rest stops and roadside gas stations. He couldn't think of the last one he passed, or even when the last time a car had blown by. With the snow and the fake light of suspended time, it felt like he and his daughter were the last two people on earth.

Just then, a soft tune, the *tink* of metal on wine glasses, played across the blizzard. It felt surreal, like a dream lingering on the edge of your mind and for a brief heartbeat you question its validity. Sullivan didn't know if he imagined it or not.

Then he definitely heard it again.

Towards the east, across the decrepit fence that ran parallel to the highway, just beyond the shoulder.

Civilization.

He hoisted his daughter across the wire and slat fence, ignoring the increased pain in his leg that caused, careful to avoid catching bulky wrappings on metal-thorn barbed wire. His precious cargo he had been entrusted with, that he almost lost in a vapor.

His chest shuddered and he choked on dry, hollow-cold air as he considered the grisly outcome if he had veered an inch to the left or the right. They should've been injured more in the crash. Something kept him, kept his daughter safe. Something out there. He looked to the snow-illuminated sky and thanked whatever watched over them during these last critical minutes.

A stir of wind responded and aspen leaves shook a dull glitter.

As the two followed the ghostly music, perception became suspended in winter-white. A minute held still, measured in numbered flakes gently cascading. A deceived eye could make a mile no more than a foot away, reachable if grasped at with numb fingertips.

The sound of music faded, replaced by a light in the distance, across a gentle slope where trees grew thin and sparse, allowing swaths of white to cover earth. The faint yellow pushed through limbs, giving the hint of a large lightning bug hiding just beyond the tree line, waiting.

Shelter may be there.

"Come on," he dug into Felly's oversized sleeve until he found her gentle hand. He clutched it tightly, leeching some of her warmth. With it he was reminded just how cold he had become. "Let's go," he said with new urgency as he pictured himself freezing to death, leaving Felly alone in the wilderness with a popsicle father. She didn't deserve that.

They made their way down the slope. Four times Felly stumbled on obscured rocks, kept aloft only by Sullivan's tight grip on her tiny arm. One time she broke away as a winding, stubborn root claimed her shoe. Sullivan slid into a painful split as his daughter's weight was enough to throw him off balance. They both crashed into snow. Any other time they would've laughed, but not with their life perched on a freezing line.

Sullivan scrambled to lift her from the wet snow so she wouldn't get any wetter than necessary. He brushed off her blanket with a ferocity and swiftness like she just landed on a bed of stinging ants. "There," he breathed as the last clumps of snow broke away from her shoulders. "You're not cold, are you?"

She shook her head. "Are you?"

Like the unresponsive Life-Sav, Sullivan didn't answer. He'd made a promise a year ago to never lie to his family again, not after his wife found him in the worst of lies in the worst kind of betrayal. He started walking again.

With each step, his dress shoes sucked in every last ounce of icy cold. His slacks were made of sponges and were licking dry every wild flower he brushed against. His teeth gave intermittent chatters when a particularly spine-tingling chill swept up his back. His chest ached as he fought to not shatter his teeth away.

Yes, Felly, he wanted to tell her, *Da is freezing to death.* Instead, he flashed her a smile she could interpret however she needed. Cold comfort.

They trudged until the slope gently leveled. Sullivan paused as he heard another sound on the wind that shouldn't have been there. At first he thought it was a continuation of the music, but then came to the conclusion it was something worse.

There, again, on the wind, a choked voice.

He closed his eyes, made himself stop shivering, listening with new intensity, beyond the heartbeat thrum in his ears. Yes, he heard it distinctly, once he searched it out.

"Help!"

His heart became fearful as he glanced to his daughter. "Do you hear?" he asked.

She gave him a momentary quizzical stare as her young mind processed. Her eyes lit with understanding. "Someone's needing help."

"Help!"

Louder now, and a million thoughts raced through Sullivan's head on what could be happening. He scanned the surrounding woods, squinting to see back towards his crashed SUV, but it wasn't in sight anymore.

"Help me!"

"This way," Sullivan tugged his daughter and darted in the direction he thought the voice came from. He ducked his head as he crashed through a faint cluster of bell-bottom spruces, their bluish forms breaking up the white. Branches raked against his face and yanked at his arms. He tightened his grip on his daughter. On the other side of the cluster, he came to a sliding halt, almost spilling forward.

A plastic layer of ice covered a pond, about sixty feet across. Groups of various-size spruces stood around the banks, vagrant Christmas trees keeping watch.

Near the middle of the pond the ice had cracked and split into bobbing floes. The voice came from among the floes, thrashing wildly. "Can't swim! Help!"

A boy was in the freezing water.

Sullivan glanced at his daughter. She watched the boy's plight unfold as a sick play performed before the drunk trees and all creation.

He had to act, even if it meant putting himself in more danger. He couldn't let this boy drown. Or freeze. "Hold on a minute, I'll save you." He released Felly's hand and began removing his light, completely inappropriate for cold weather clothes. "I have to help," he reassured himself and his daughter.

Several crackles and pops indicated the flailing boy broke up more ice in his panic. It sounded like wood planks split by an ogre.

After Sullivan kicked off his shoes, he debated with himself on taking his socks off. It seemed like he took way too long to make this simple decision. "I'm sorry, I'm hurrying," he apologized.

Wrapping his thin arms around his torso, he rushed to the edge of the pond, where the ground and frozen water became indistinguishable from each in the wintery storm, searching the rim for the best way to enter.

Another man was on the opposite side of the pond.

Sullivan hadn't noticed him before because he was wearing some kind of full-body suit, off-white, and was splayed on top of the ice, blending into the background. He inched across, closing in on the boy. "Hold on, I'll help!" Sullivan yelled out, but the man didn't respond.

There was no good spot to enter from Sullivan's vantage point.

The man reached the boy, and within a couple minutes, was sliding backward, dragging the boy he somehow salvaged from the water. "Stay here," Sullivan said to his daughter before running around the pond, adrenaline warming him from inside. But by the time he reached the man, he had already completed the rescue. On the pond's edge, the man sat cross-legged on frozen ground, the cold, waterlogged boy resting in his arms, an impromptu *Pietà*.

On closer inspection, Sullivan could see the man was of Asian descent. So was the boy. He quickly and efficiently surmised by their resemblance they were father and son. "Does he need CPR?" he asked as he ran through the ABCs of life-saving techniques, but the man didn't respond. He kept his eyes focused on the boy in his arms.

He whispered in the boy's ear in another language. Even though Sullivan couldn't understand the words, he knew the tone. It's the prayer of a nervous father waiting for the delivery of his first child. It's a mother's tender reassurance a scraped knee isn't bad.

It's a man hoping to pluck his son from the greedy hands of Death by hope and prayers.

"Is he alright?" Sullivan asked again, but again, the man didn't respond.

The boy sputtered and coughed, then began a long, mournful wail that challenged the whipping blizzard in intensity. The man clutched the boy closer and got to his feet.

Sullivan, standing near naked in the snow, as the adrenaline subsided, became keenly aware of his body beginning a new round of tremors. "Hold on," he held a finger up like that alone would keep time stalled. "I'll be right back. Let me get my clothes back on." He zipped back around the pond. He looked over his shoulder in time to see the man making his way up the opposite slope, his white-clothed figure quickly becoming lost in white. "Hold on!" he yelled and gave himself an extra burst of speed to reach Felly, patiently waiting, just like he'd told her.

He fumbled for his clothes with fingers refusing to cooperate, punishing him for letting them get so cold. Fingertips tingled in painful delight. He cursed under his breath as he wrestled with one pant leg somehow twisted in a knot.

"Da, what of the people," Felly said, looking from him to the pond. "Did the boy die?"

Sullivan was stricken to the core when he heard her ask that question. It's a moment you dread as a parent but realize is inevitable. Your child you've worked so hard to protect is growing up in a world that doesn't care she was two weeks premature or that peanuts throw her into anaphylactic shock.

The world doesn't care and makes her ask such tough questions as did someone die.

"No, not die," he reassured her. "We need to catch up to them. Come on." He began a fast-walk around the pond even before his shoes were tied. After several steps of clenching his toes to keep his frozen shoes from falling off, he halted, bent. He tied the strings in a rough knot. Standing upright, he grasped Felly's sleeve. "Come on."

The last of the adrenaline passed, so winter in all its fury filled back in with icy tendrils. Sullivan wrapped his one free arm around his torso, more as mental reassurance than for any real benefit.

When the two reached the opposite slope, the man had disappeared. That put Sullivan into a panic. “Where?” as he unintentionally yanked his daughter’s arm, almost knocking her over. He couldn't find them.

As consolation, though, or something more, his eyes were driven to a faint set of footprints winding up the slope. He could’ve easily overlooked them, had it not been for the odd twilight illuminating them.

He set after them with renewed hope.

The father and daughter made their way up the slope, almost stepping foot-to-foot in the prints left by the Asian man. The night-but-not-night ambient light made the fading footprints glow with a thin blue life of their own. They followed the trail, circling around a grove of scraggly aspens, their pockmarked trunks creating a natural fence line.

Around the trees, they emerged onto a maze of hedges about waist-high. It spanned out for about fifty yards, and at the other end was a three-story Victorian, covered in vines dormant for the winter.

It appeared like a tree had been planted upside down underneath the house and its roots had engulfed the structure. But the amazing part wasn't the house or the upside-down tree, it was in the center of the hedge maze.

A boy, an adolescent, about twelve or so, gripped a pair of silver hedge clippers. He wore a wide brim straw-weave hat, shorts, and no shirt. In the cold.

"Excuse me, hello?" Sullivan said, his statement morphing into a question as the boy seemed oblivious to the two. He stopped about fifteen feet from the hard-working junior gardener.

The boy was lost in a world of icy dust blossoms. He hummed in tune with each sharp snap of his silver clippers. It was the tune Sullivan had heard earlier.

"Da, why's he doing that in the snow?" Felly asked.

"I don't know." Sullivan shivered, put off by the boy's oblivious winter-time gardening. "Come, Felly, let's see if we can make it inside."

The two skirted the boy and easily navigated the rest of the maze, which let out in front of a massive full arch double leaf door. It reminded Sullivan of the entrance to the old run-down church just down the street from his studio apartment, full of wooden ornamentation and stained glass.

He grasped the brass knocker and a cold shock rippled through his hand. He jerked his hand away from the unexpected frigidness and instinctively clutched it to his chest, cradling the wound tenderly.

The door swung inward under its own power.

"Hello," Sullivan said as he poked his head inside.

A warmth seeped from the house, welcoming them. Disregarding etiquette, Sullivan ushered his daughter and himself inside.

The door closed under its own power.

They stood just inside a room that was more like a grand hallway, spanning far greater that it had appeared from outside. Sullivan felt they'd just tumbled across a threshold of reality into a dream-state world of impossibility.

The one room consolidated several rooms. They were in a section that resembled a living area, a plush couch of crushed red velvet faced a crackling fireplace. A grand mantle of mahogany arched over the top, crowded with an urn, an ornate box, and small metal trinkets. Softly, at the back of the nose, he could smell freshly-cooked oak. It warmed Sullivan from the inside out, the way piping chicken noodle soup wipes away childhood colds.

He sat his daughter near the fire on an ottoman painted with rich and vibrant beads twisting in an amalgam of vibrant colors, gold tassels dangling off the sides.

He rubbed his hands, kicked his soggy shoes and socks off, then rubbed his toes that had already lost sensation. The fire-heat in his feet exploded in prickles of thawing pain and he winced and jerked his feet away from the fire.

As he warmed, he inspected the rest of the long room.

The living section translated to a section that appeared to have been used by an architect, or an artist. A drafting table was pushed against a wall. A four-tier shelf held a myriad of pencils corralled by holders and open cigar boxes. Several paperboard cylinders had been stacked against the wall in the shape of a half tee pee. Butcher block paper had been taped to a wall, undecipherable schematics covering the surface.

"Welcome, stranger," a voice echoed from a hallway half way down the room. An old, yet lively, voice. Sullivan detected hints of an Asian accent, but his only baseline to determine this was from Hollywood's interpretation of minor-role ethnic characterizations. Or the man outside.

"Uhm, hello," he quickly tried to stuff his left foot back in a wet sock. "We ran off the road. I needed to get my daughter—"

"No, no," the kindly voice soothed. "Please, sit. It is quite a storm out."

Around the corner came an old man, an old Asian man, to match the voice. He wore a long-sleeved shirt that appeared more like a thermal liner. His back was slightly hunched and he didn't quite pick his feet up as he walked. His soft-soled shoes made a *swoof* with each step.

"Outside," Sullivan said as he remembered, pointing behind him to emphasize, "There was a boy in a pond."

Without any sense of care the man waved his hands dismissively. "He's fine." He made his way to the two and gave a slight bow as he came to a shuffling stop. "I'm most honored to have you visit me. Providence has brought you here."

Sullivan pulled his phone from his pocket, hoping it'd register a signal. "I tried to call for help."

"I imagine it didn't work. Sorry about all that."

Just then, laughter and footsteps on linoleum exploded into the room as a boy, about Felly's age, deftly positioned himself behind the couch. He peered over an armrest to the hallway he'd just come from.

A man followed after him, puffing heavily. He stopped, scanned the room in an exaggerated manner with his hand cupped over his eyes like shielding them from the sun. He roared as his eyes locked in the boy.

The boy squealed in childhood playfulness and bolted from his spot and out the room. The man followed.

They carried on like they never saw Sullivan or his daughter, or even the old man. He just watched the two like it was completely normal, a smile on his face.

Now that Sullivan studied the old man, he was an older version of the man chasing the boy. In fact, the boy here looked like the boy outside. "What in the…" Sullivan said.

"I used to love playing chase with my dad," the old man said, a wistful look passing across his wrinkles. "I think I kept him running for days." He chuckled, memories before his eyes.

"Was that your son and grandson, then?" Sullivan asked, sure he'd solved the mystery.

"Oh no. That boy is me."

Sullivan did a double take.

The old man took a seat on the red couch. "There was a time when I awoke in my lonely condo, leaving the dream world of impossibility, when the unnatural is exchanged for the natural, the unreal for the real. Where you live each moment in a discordant, jagged flow of modular haphazard scenes of stitched together memory, interspersed with bed-time tosses and continual searching for the cool side of the pillow." He said this like he'd repeated this mantra to himself each day for the past ten years. A penance for some past sin forgotten except in his mind.

He continued. "And from my dreams is where it all started. There, I'd begun to wonder, prompted by the impossibility of that nether world, I'd asked one simple question...

"What if I could make a living entity—a person—out of silicone and solid state? What if I could create life, whatever life was? A self-actualized being, that's what life is, that's what separates us from animals. We're aware of ourselves, our actions. We think; therefore, we are. Driven by a divine spark.

"What if I can be that divine spark?"

He paused to take a breath. Sullivan didn't know what to say so he didn't say anything.

"You see," the man said after collecting more thoughts. "I founded Masanori Intelligence. The preeminent leader in adaptive cognition. I made computers think like humans. And with each processor upgrade, each new advanced solid state replacement, they thought faster, better."

Sullivan shook his head in disbelief. "You're kidding. *The* Masanori Nishimora? Everyone thinks you've crawled in a hole and died."

Masanori didn't seem to notice Sullivan anymore. "Age has a way of bending youthful preconceptions. When the *might be* is replaced with the *as it is*, you find those youthful preconceptions often are just that, juvenile. Life flitted by while I pursued building the perfect man. And I found myself alone."

Sullivan snapped his fingers as he recollected a grocery store tabloid he'd skimmed over last summer as he was drawn in by cover spreads of a Kardashian. "I thought you'd made a wife. There were those reports: BILLIONAIRE MOGUL MAKES PERFECT AMERICAN WIFE OUT OF SPARE PARTS."

"Yes," Masanori nodded. "A beautiful woman, with Western eyes and the figure of a supermodel. I heard the outrage from the Asian community when I supposedly gave her

American-white skin, slightly tan, instead of keeping her looking Japanese. It was all manufactured nonsense, sensationalism, bait in order for you to click.

"Sure I could've done that. Physical traits are the easy part. Now the mind," he tapped his temple, "that's the trick. Don't you see, there was no divine spark. I've been creating extravagant puppets. Marionettes for the masses."

He looked at Felly. "You have what I desired the most but couldn't make: a beautiful child. At one time, I'm sure you've had a wife at best, a passing relationship at worst."

"I have a wife," Sullivan admonished, then stopped as he needed to correct his soon-to-be lie. "Well, we're separated now, but we were married for ten years. You," He added, "you had a son, right?"

"No," Masanori responded. "My son is a fancy wind-up toy. The little boy is me, not my son. Those are memories of me with my father. Another time, another place."

"Then," Sullivan's frost-addled mind thawed with understanding, "the boy in the pond…"

"Yes, I almost died that day, if it weren't for dad."

"And the boy in the garden…"

Masanori laughed. "Every summer I tended neighborhood gardens. My first job."

"Those are all you."

"My memories, played out like a ballerina on a music box. A memory play. I'd missed life while trying to create life. Funny, huh. This is my humble attempt at remembering, creating androids to replay my memories. But I must apologize for keeping you from being able to use your phone. I've had to disrupt telecom signals around the house. Paparazzi, you know."

He stood, which appeared to be a great effort on his part and went to the mantle. Pushing aside the urn to give him space, he gingerly took the ornate box. The gem-encrusted cover glistened as firelight played across the surface. He wiped dust off with a sleeve before handing it to Felly. "Here, for inconveniencing you so."

Felly looked to her father, waiting for his approving nod like a dog waiting to dig into his food. Sullivan nodded and Felly eagerly grabbed the box.

"Open it," Masanori said.

Felly did. The top lifted open to reveal a ballerina frozen in an *Arabesque penchée*; one leg extended behind her stiffly, head forward, arms gracefully held. Music, the tinker-box music

Sullivan had heard in the snow-covered field, played.

"*Invitation to the Dance*," Masanori whispered.

The ballerina spun as she glided along the figure eight track on the mirrored music box surface. She'd do this forever.

"The last of my mother's possessions," Masanori said. "I'd saved it for my child that never came. And what would an android do with a music box?"

"Thank you," Sullivan said.

Masanori glanced at his watch. He sighed. "I was aware of your accident when it happened. I called a tow truck. By now one should be tending to your vehicle. It's paid for already."

Thanking Masanori again, Sullivan put on his clothes that were reasonably dry from the partial baking in front of the fireplace. He checked Felly over, making sure her jacket was buttoned. She clutched the music box in her arms.

The door opened under its own power.

"I hope you find peace with your androids," Sullivan said as they left the house.

The father and daughter trudged into the snow and headed to the crashed SUV where Providence waited for them. Sullivan had an overwhelming urge to talk to Patricia. Maybe they could sit down for dinner together when he dropped off Felly. There was a lot to discuss.

Masanori watched as they disappeared into the approaching night.

He shuffled back to the mantle, picked up the urn. He read the brass plate affixed to the side: MASANORI NISHIMORA, FATHER OF ANDROIDS, R.I.P.

"I've already found my peace," he said before wiping dust off the urn with his sleeve. He placed it back on the mantle.

The End

A.K. Meek

A mild-mannered management engineer by day, a mild-mannered writer by night. A.K. writes speculative, slipstream science fiction and fantasy. He has penned alternate realities where robots are treated as gods fallen to earth, built cities filled to the brim with artificial animals, and crafted stories of alien invaders that can see human thought. He has also dipped his hand in "Jericho" style post-apocalyptic fiction and birthed a fantastic world where truth and lie can occupy the same space. He lives in the Deep South, among the mosquitoes and magnolias, with his wonderful wife and menagerie of dogs and cats, and a wild rabbit that occasionally strays into the back yard for a visit.

See what he's up to on Facebook at: http://www.facebook.com/authorakmeek/

and Instagram at: http://www.instagram.com/akmeek/

Join his reader group to get new and free stuff. Who doesn't like free stuff? You can't lose! http://www.akmeek.com/newsletter

Unerella

Keturah Lamb

Once there was a very pretty girl. She could have made a great lady if only her skin were clean and powdered, her hair styled high on her head, and her clothes fancy and fine. But instead she was an orphan, fated to live with her strict aunt and uncle and six younger cousins – all of which were very dirty and ornery.

Calista dreamed of a better life as she chased, scrubbed, and watched her cousins. She dreamed of a life with good parents, easier, pleasanter work. A life where the house wasn't always dirty, the fire always cold. She also dreamed of ways she'd help others like her have an easier life. But most of all, Calista dreamed of finding true love.

She did not care if he were rich or poor, just as long as he loved her. Of course, it would be nice if he were rich. For then he could make her life less miserable. And she would have less work and pain, and many, many pretty things.

Even if he were poor, though, he would still find ways to splurge on her, for Calista's man would love her very much. Though she dreamed all day amidst her piles of dished heaps of chores, she never imagined any of her fantasies coming true. They were, after all, just fantasies.

Until now.

"If only I..."

"Who was here?" Calista's aunt snapped, breaking into the girl's pleasant thoughts.

"A squire." Calista smiled, at her aunt, still not back to earth. "He said all girls are attend a three-day banquet for the Prince."

"Ha! This the reason for your stupor?" Her aunt knuckled Calista on the head. "Get out of it! There's work to be done. Ain't neither of us time for parties."

Anger and frustrations coupled with the pain and previous mistreatments welled up inside of her. But Calista tried to keep her temper in check. "The squire said all girls are to attend."

She regretted her words after receiving another smack. Her face reddened under the pain, and her tears did not make her feel better.

"Have it your way. Go. Humiliate yourself. What do I care? But don't try to get us to buy you clothes. And don't be disappointed when the prince can't even see you."

"Thank you so much, Auntie!"

Her Aunt humphed and walked out of the kitchen. "Just make sure to finish your work on time, and don't neglect the boys, or I'll make sure you can't go."

Broom in hand, Calista spun around the kitchen, continuing her work at a slower pace as she daydreamed. She had stared often in her aunt's mirror. When washed and ready for market she was never sore to look at. In fact, she was far from that. But was that enough? She had little to her name.

Yet, why shouldn't the Prince love her?

Here was her chance!

"I can practice being graceful without fear of being mocked. And if the prince were to choose me–oh, but then a new life would be mine!"

Her lonely heart ached to go, to be loved. If only...

No, she would hope with all her heart! No doubting would enter.

Her cousins entered the kitchen at that moment, covered with mud, laughing over some game.

"Boys, what would your mother say!" They hushed as they became aware of their filthy clothes. No one said a word. The littlest one tried to hide his sheepish grin.

Calista laughed. "Come on. We'll get you all cleaned up!"

#

"When is the ball?"

Calista scrubbed her little cousin almost viciously, his skin a bright red from the lye soap. She had to talk to someone – so she had been telling him everything she knew and even more about what she imagined the ball to be like.

"It begins next week!" Calista answered the little boy. She poured another handful of suds in his hair and scrubbed his long curls with her finger nails scraping against his scalp.

"What will you wear, Calista?"

The girl's smile vanished suddenly. Her wet hands fell to her lap. It was a fantasy. She couldn't go. Not without a dress.

What had she been thinking?

"I don't know." A tear escaped from her eye and fell into the wooden tub, making a small splash.

#

In market the next day Calista still couldn't get over her disappointment. Normally these days to town were great fun and a delightful escape from home.

But today, as she compared it all to her splendid dreams, everything was dull.

Calista did her bartering subconsciously.

She didn't search for bargains, and when she did happen upon good deals, she didn't feel her normal thrill of pride. She simply bought what she needed, sticking it in her basket, not caring at all.

At the same moment she left one table for another, trumpets sounded close by. She looked up curiously, her thoughts dissolving for the moment.

"Make way for the Prince!" A squire shouted as he stepped out of the prince's carriage. "Your Prince wishes to visit this market and its humble citizens. Refrain from approaching him, unless directed otherwise."

He never passed this way! What was he doing in this market? In her town?

Something fluttered throughout Calista's insides as she watched the Prince climb out of his carriage. His smile held so much kindness, surely meant for all the town. His handsome face sent Calista into an enraptured trance so that he was all she could see.

Her infatuation for him grew as she watched him dirty his hands by helping an older lady pick up her basket of apples.

"I'm sorry if my horses scared you." He bowed slightly to the lady.

Calista sighed. His voice was rich, deep, perfect – the best thing she had ever heard.

The lady laughed, as if a young, giddy girl.

He inspected the people's produce and wares, buying something small from many of the booths, giving more than the asking price.

He was walking towards her!

Calista made herself breathe as he stopped before her, smiling. He looked right into her eyes, "Good day, my lady."

Had he just called her a lady? Calista wanted to laugh with excitement, but she kept herself together and just nodded her head, "My Prince."

He took her hand and kissed it. At that moment Calista wasn't sure if she were living real life or dreaming another fantasy. Her hand felt so dead and a live at once, full of some strange sensation.

"Thank you, my lord." She felt a surge of pride as she curtsied with natural grace.

Oh, the whole town had to be looking at her right now! She wasn't full of dread, but joy. Was this love?

He looked directly back at her, waving to all, as he boarded his carriage, finally leaving.

Her mind was made up. She would go to the ball.

Nothing would stop her.

Nothing.

She walked straight to the dressmaker's. Once outside she felt scared – dare she enter? She came here often because she loved looking at the soft materials and beautiful gowns – but it was different this time. She forced a breath and walked in.

"Hello," Calista said a little too loudly.

"Hello, Calista! How are you doing this fine morning?"

Her fear disappeared and she smiled. "I am doing well – and you?"

The dressmaker nodded, her face kind. "What might I help you with?"

Calista sent a look around the room. There were so many pretty pieces of clothing, so many long cloths that seemed to dance with color. "I'd like a dress for the ball – I plan to marry the prince."

She winced even as she said the words. So confident – what if the prince planned otherwise? But she told herself that hope was good. And he had already shown her special attention. That was enough.

"I don't have any money, though." Calista looked at the floor suddenly feeling foolish.

A moment of silence passed before the dressmaker said, "That's alright, my dear. Just come over her and let me get your measurements. You can pay me back by working for me, if need be."

Calista smiled. "If I marry the prince I'll be able to pay you more than it's worth."
The dressmaker sent Calista a warm smile.

#

The first night of the ball arrived. Calista was all ready. Her aunt scoffed at her excitement, but the little boys were jumping up and down singing, "Calista will marry the prince! Calista will marry the prince!"

Calista blushed. She hadn't out right said that she would marry him, but maybe it was obvious to everyone already that she had a very good chance.

Just look at her dress!

Calista twirled as her cousins admired it. The skirt was full, cascading smoothly to the floor. The satin sparkled against the fire light, making the rich blue look even more shiny. The dress fit perfectly – the neckline scooped down just enough, the sleeves fit her shoulders outlining her small figure. All the ruffles bounced and danced.

A neighboring pumpkin farmer offered her a ride to the castle. He talked the whole way. Calista wondered how anyone could speak on a night like this.

But he had a lot to say – about how this was a wonderful opportunity for her, and that even if she didn't get the prince, maybe she would find some other nice gentleman.

"You don't think the prince will like me?" Calista asked anxiously.

"He'd be loony not to," was the reply. "But ye never ken tell about men and who'll they'll fancy. Even if he doesn't, remember you are still the pertiest gal I know."

"As pretty as your wife?" Calista teased.

"Nah, ye know what I meant. The pertiest young 'un."

She laughed. Other than that, she didn't hear much of what he said. She was too caught up in the excitement of the night.

"Well, there ye are."

As Calista looked up at the magnificent place, her heart swelled with excitement.

As she walked up the to the doors, she prayed, so nervous. Of all the girls out there, she deserved a happy future. Didn't she? She needed this – him – so badly. She loved the prince already.

It had been love at first sight.

And she couldn't imagine life any different. Without him – what would life be? Calista shuddered. No. The reason life looked blank without him was because it would be. She and the prince were meant to be together.

#

Calista entered the castle. Already so many people were here. She pasted on a smile, and walked in, tall, full of put-on confidence.

She looked around for the prince. Would he remember her from last week? He had to, if it had been true love.

The prince noticed Calista right off, putting her fears to rest, his eyes widening as soon as he saw her.

Calista saw him walking to her, reaching her swiftly. She had been right! He did love her!

Soon they were dancing and talking and laughing. She'd never been so happy before. Never felt so loved.

When he danced with the other girls she noted – or imagined – that he seemed bored and disinterested. But with Calista his eyes sparkled and he always smiled.

Of course, none of the other girls could care for him like she did, she told herself. Each of them must have only come for the excitement. She was sure they all had wonderful suitors at home already, unlike herself.

But what made this more certain in her

mind was that he danced with her the most. At least this is what she thought. There were quite a few other girls that claimed the same thing after the ball, but whether they spoke the truth or not was very questionable, for Calista did dance often with the prince.

Until an hour after the ball had begun.

She entered in so unexpectedly and suddenly. She was as dainty as a China doll – daintier if possible. Her grace was surreal, airy.

"Who is she?" All of the girls whispered.

"Look at her dress!" It was made out of some unknown delicate material that appeared to be ready to fly away at any moment. It almost looked like it had been made of butterfly wings.

"What are those slippers made of?"

"Glass?"

"No!"

"Wait, they are!!"

Calista could feel the prince's eyes turn to the strange girl. Something stirred inside of him. And it wasn't for Calista. His grip on her loosened. She couldn't feel his body warmth any more.

"Who is she?" someone asked again.

The prince forgot Calista was at his side, letting go of her hands. His face was drained of color, as if the sight of this new girl put him in shock.

He walked away, straight for *her*–the China doll.

The prince didn't dance with Calista again that night.

#

She cried silently on the way home. Once home, Calista jumped from the wagon and ran to the house. Calista sighed in relief despite her tears. Everyone was asleep. She wouldn't have to face anyone tonight. She slipped out of her dress, hanging it on a nail. She stared at her dress dismally. It was supposed to be the start of a new life. What had happened?

She crawled into bed, crying harder. Oh, what a night! True love couldn't just end like that, could it? Her heart still clung to hope. Maybe tomorrow would be better… but still she cried herself to sleep.

The next morning things looked better. She told herself it was a dream. Tonight the prince would love her again. Convinced of this unreality, she answered the boys accordingly.

Her aunt said little except "Mind you don't get too high and mighty to finish your chores."

The farmer again gave her a ride to the castle. She ran inside hoping the prince would be waiting – with arms open for her.

But the mysterious woman of the night before was already there, dancing with the prince.

She managed to have one dance that night. But their conversation wasn't near as charming or fulfilling as it had been the previous night. He was continually looking over to where the China doll stood. And once the dance was over, he barely said a thank you before running back to *her* side.

As the prince was dancing with another girl, Calista and the delicate mystery lady happened to be at the refreshment table together.

She smiled at Calista sweetly, and asked her about herself. Calista found herself forgetting about the prince and slowly growing to like the girl as they chatted. And then she remembered that she was her rival.

Or was she? Did she not also want to be happy? Who deserved the prince more?

Why must this girl's happiness be fulfilled through Calista's expense?

On the third night the prince danced with no one else save the petite and pretty girl. Silent tears escaped Calista's eyes every so often. She sat in a lonely corner watching the prince and the China doll, mourning her true love.

"Hello?" a man's voice broke into her thoughts, forcing her to turn away from her lost love to look at another. "Why is someone as pretty as you standing all alone?"

"I am enjoying the scenery," she lied, forcing a fake smile.

The man smiled, "Will you dance with me?"

Calista panicked. She would not give up on her prince so easily. "I'm sorry, but I am actually occupied at the moment."

The man's eyes widened slightly with surprise. He gave a short bow, "Of course." And walked away.

She watched him dissolve into the crowd, feeling just a little guilty.

There were several other men that spoke to Calista but she would have nothing to do with any of them. And the other girls were all too happy, appearing foolish to Calista. She left early when an appropriate time arose, wrapped in her sorrow.

"I'll never love anyone else!" She cried. Calista forced herself to leave her bed and dress in her old clothing. She imagined the lonely, hard life ahead of her. Her aunt had no mercy. Her uncle did not care about her and only gave her a home out of duty. The boys could be sweet, but any more they were just a complete nuisance.

Life held nothing for her anymore. Just work and no joy.

She was sobbing uncontrollably when she reached the kitchen.

The boys sat around the fire. The littlest one ran to her when he saw she was crying. "What is it, Calista?"

"Leave me alone!" she snapped through her tears. But she held on to him tightly.

Her aunt entered the room. She was about to open her mouth to scold the girl, but then turned to go for some odd reason. Calista did not feel like figuring out the reason. Maybe her aunt was able to feel mercy after all. At least on this one occasion.

#

A week later news drifted around the neighborhood and town that the pretty, mysterious China doll woman was missing. Calista's heart jumped to her throat when she heard. If the other girl was never found, then there was a chance that the prince would return for her. He would have to remember his first and true love.

One of the glass slippers had been found. A squire went around from door to door requesting all ladies to try it on. Calista did so willingly, for whoever it would fit, that was the one the prince would marry. And though her foot was too large, she still didn't give up hope. Maybe they never would find a foot that fit the slipper. It was insanely small, after all.

But they did find the mysterious girl–Cinderella. And once the prince had her back, it wasn't long afterward they married.

Calista cried harder during the wedding celebration than she ever had before. Her sorrow was even worse than before. The wound that had barely healed had been opened too soon and cut deeper. The passion she'd felt was replaced with a pain that seemed would never be able to heal. She wanted to die—but life was meant to continue on. A new day started. Calista forced herself to rise early and wash her face, braid her hair, and try on a smile. She would return the dress to the dressmaker's.

As she walked to town she heard rumors of a sweet story passed between person to person.

"They say the Prince's bride was nothing but a servant – to her own family."

"What a beautiful story – evidence that how true love may be found no matter the circumstances."

"They say it was almost magical the way she was even able to attend. As if fate couldn't have it any other way."

"Proof that dreams do come true – just have faith!"

Calista wanted to laugh bitterly at all the words. People would use this story as an example. But what about her? Were her dreams not big enough? Her hope not nearly as strong? What about all the other girls that attended the ball? Only one girl won the prince.

Didn't she deserve his love just as much as that beautiful girl? Yet, here she was the opposite of Cinderella–an Unerella.

She reached the dressmaker's shop, opening the door much slower than she had the first time.

She looked at her reflection in the shop mirror. Her eyes appeared tired, but at least they were dry and not swollen.

"Hello, Calista," the dressmaker quietly said.

Calista felt glad the dressmaker did not ask how she was doing. She would not have known how to answer. "I have the dress. I've come to return it and talk about payment." She felt so much stronger as she spoke, though her heart still ached.

The woman took the dress. "It looks just as it did when I gave it to you – you took great care of it."

"Thank you." Of course, she hadn't danced much after the first night – just stood and watched. So, it only made sense the dress still looked new. "How much do I owe you?"

The dressmaker thought a moment, "I don't normally loan dresses out -"

"Loan?" Calista asked, puzzled.

The dressmaker continued as if Calista hadn't interrupted her, "I'm not sure what a fair price would be, but I am sure we can work something out. How good are you with a needle?"

Calista answered, "Decently. I mend all my cousins clothing and make my own."

"Very good – how does a week of working here at the shop sound?"

Calista wasn't sure how to answer. Life was so hopeless. But now it was as if a light were trying to break free into her dark world. She could actually do something to regain purpose – all she had to do was accept.

"And if you enjoy the work—and we both enjoy each other's company I shall consider taking you on as an apprentice. I have much more work than I used to have, and I have been thinking of hiring a girl for some time now."

Calista still felt betrayed by the prince. Her pain still dwelt inside. But she was finally able to smile. "I like that," Calista answered.

"When do you want me to start?"

The End

Keturah Lamb is a young woman learning how to both live in and embrace God's reality. The written and verbal words help this process. She likes to call herself a realistic idealist. She has many passions in life, the first being her ideas concerning friendship {love}, the second being laughter {smile}. She grew up in Missouri and currently lives in Montana but travels several times a year to visit friends who live too far away. Though her first love is writing, she cleans houses as she strongly believes artists shouldn't starve. You can read more of her work at http://keturahskorner.blogspot.com/ where she posts every Wednesday.

Mark the Days

Kat Heckenbach

Denver blinked against the sunlight blaring through his bedroom window, resisting the urge to pull the thick comforter over his face. Moments later, the sunlight shut off. He blinked more, seeing nothing but pitch black for several seconds. As his eyes adjusted to the dark, the furniture in his room appearing as deeper shadows, he noticed the hum of an engine coming from outside.

Blast it, Jerry. Denver groaned and flipped over on his stomach, scrunching his eyes shut again. Why could his housemate never remember to park on the other side when he came home at this time of morning? His headlights lined up exactly with Denver's window, sending blinding light through the curtains.

The engine cut off, and soon the front lock clicked, followed by the slam of the door against the wall. Then the clomp of Jerry's boots down the hardwood floor of the hallway that led to Jerry's room on the other side of the house.

Denver lifted his head and glanced over at the clock. Three-thirty. He exhaled, glad he at least wouldn't have to deal with Jerry in the morning. Jerry would sleep in, not arising until long after Denver headed to the office. Then he'd be gone again when Denver got home. Jerry working nights meant Denver had the house to himself most evenings. Simple blessings...

The alarm blasted Denver from a heavy sleep, and he grunted as he slammed the off button. Shoving the comforter aside, he dragged himself over to the edge of the bed. When his feet hit the floor, he let out a sigh. Mornings sucked. Even more so with lack of sleep.

When he reached the kitchen, the barest hint of sunrise lit the window, enough to see the coffee maker. He switched it on, listening to the gurgle of heating water with anticipation. While he waited, he snagged a marker from the mug on the counter and marked off the day on the calendar.

Jerry's snicker startled him, and he spun around to find Jerry slouched over the breakfast bar, coffee in hand. Denver's own cup sat steaming on the counter top. The room was brighter than five-thirty would allow.

How—?

Denver rubbed his forehead. Had he dozed off standing there?

"Dude," Jerry said, "you okay?" His blond hair flopped over one eye, and he brushed it back, only to have it flop again.

"What? Yeah. Fine." But Denver didn't feel fine. He looked at the calendar he'd just marked. May fifteenth. That wasn't right. He'd skipped a day.

Jerry snickered again. "I know, I know. You're fine as long as your little ritual is done. Mark each day, every day. Perfect little X over the number..." He shook his head, eye peeking intermittently from behind his swinging bangs.

Denver stared at the calendar, the number 14 clearly visible with no perfect little X. "You see everything marked through today?" he asked, hoping the alarm didn't show in his voice.

"Of course." Jerry slid from the barstool and dumped his mug into the sink. As he walked past, he elbowed Denver's arm. "What's wro—I mean..." His voice dropped. "Never mind." He didn't say anything more and ducked through the door that led from the kitchen to the back porch. Which would make sense if it were May fifteenth because the fifteenth was Wednesday, Jerry's day off. He only slept in on the days he had to work.

How was it May fifteenth, though?

Denver picked up his coffee mug. The muscle in his arm twitched where Jerry's bony elbow had hit him. He rubbed it with his other hand, and his touch was met with unfamiliar slick fabric. He looked down at his shirt. It was one of those t-shirts made of moisture-wicking material. But Denver didn't own one of those shirts. Much less a purple one.

He grabbed his coffee and downed several gulps. How had he gotten this shirt? Why did he not remember putting in on? And there was something about the purple...

Another gulp of coffee, and he slammed his mug on the counter. Then he dashed to his bathroom, flipping the light on only when he was standing in front of the vanity. He stared at his sudden reflection. The purple shirt had the outline of a white teardrop in the center of the chest. No, not a tear drop. A blood drop. With a number 3 inside it. The blood drive place gave out shirts like this with each gallon milestone. Denver had red and blue, one gallon and two respectively, but those were plain cotton. He'd noticed two months ago the donation center had switched to these. Two months ago, on March fourteenth, when he was one pint away from hitting the three gallon mark and made an appointment for May fourteenth.

Had he passed out? He'd never had trouble giving blood before. Never even felt light-headed. Yet, he couldn't remember a single moment of the day before. Not waking up, not going to work. Not giving blood. Nothing. It was if he'd gone to bed Monday night and woken up on Wednesday. But he had to have woken up on Tuesday. He had on the shirt. And a small red mark stood out against the skin of the inside of his elbow. He touched the spot and found it to be tender.

"Knock, knock."

Again Denver jumped at the sound of Jerry's voice. He spun around to find Jerry slumped against the bathroom doorframe.

"Hey, I know you're proud of that shirt and all, but seriously, dude." He lifted one eyebrow. "Michelle just called. She said there were some files you need to bring today, and if you don't, something about your boys and a platter." His mouth curled into a wicked grin, then he ducked out of the room.

Before Denver had a chance to have another thought, Jerry reappeared in the doorway. The wicked grin was gone, replaced by the most somber expression Denver had seen on his friend's face. Jerry's head dropped forward as he cleared his throat. "And, um, hey…I know you made me swear to never bring it up—and I do swear not a word after this moment—but I'm praying, dude." Jerry disappeared from the doorway.

Denver stared at the empty spot where Jerry had been standing. What was that about? He almost chased after Jerry, but Michelle's words slammed him to a halt. The files were supposed to be turned in yesterday. Why hadn't

Denver done so? His job, and Michelle's, hinged on that account. He'd finished everything Monday night, crashing into bed late, which was why he'd been so ticked at Jerry for waking him up. If today really was Wednesday, and yesterday had been Tuesday, there was no way he hadn't turned in the files.

He bolted out of the bathroom and grabbed his briefcase from where it leaned against his dresser. He barely had it unzipped when he saw the folders, clearly labeled. Toch Industries.

"Crap."

The briefcase slipped from Denver's hands, hitting the carpet with a soft thud. Denver yanked his new purple shirt over his head and tossed it onto the bed, then hastily picked an outfit for work. Once he was dressed, he snatched up the briefcase and hightailed it to the office, fiercely gripping the steering wheel of his Honda Accord to stop his hands from shaking. If he didn't get those files there literally yesterday, he was a dead man.

#

Michelle was sitting at his desk, stone-faced and twirling a pair of scissors in a way that made Denver involuntarily shift his briefcase protectively in front of, as she'd so eloquently put it, his boys. The scissors stopped their movement, and Michelle tilted her head to the side. "You wanna explain all this?"

Denver stared, tongue shifting in his mouth as if searching for words, possible reasons he hadn't been to work the day before. But there were none.

His office chair creaked as Michelle pushed her weight forward so she could prop her elbows on his desk. The scissors did not leave her grasp. "You don't show up to work yesterday, then ignore every call, every text, every email. I waited for you all day. I made excuses." Her eyes narrowed. "Mr. Harrison does not like excuses."

As if Denver needed to be told that.

"Now. You. Are. Going. To. Tell. Me. Where. You've. Been."

A pain sliced through Denver's side. Not his chest, but he immediately thought heart attack and grabbed his arm. Still no words came. He had no idea where he'd been, why he hadn't come back to work. Why he'd put on his blood donation milestone shirt and worn it home without washing it first. Why he'd gone to bed wearing it. Why Jerry was praying for something he'd said in confidence and sworn Jerry not to bring up....

"Michelle, I..." It was all he could muster. He pulled the files from his still-open briefcase and laid them on the desk in front of her.

Her gaze shifted down to the file folders. The scissors, held in her left hand, lowered until their point touched the desktop. Without looking back up, she said, "When I'm done going through these, I'll let you know whether to compose a resignation letter or not."

Denver turned and left his office, the knot in his gut telling him he would not be going back except to clear out his belongings.

Which was why he stood, dumbfounded and speechless again, when Michelle called him back into his office and he found her leaning back in his chair with a smile on her face. The scissors had been returned to the mug he used as a pen holder on the corner of his desk.

"This is excellent work, Denver. I think you may have just saved yourself." She snatched the files from the desktop, stood, and marched out of his office.

Denver turned when he heard her footsteps stop.

From where Michelle stood in the hallway, without looking back at him, she added, "Don't screw up again." She continued on her way, heels clicking on the tile floor.

Denver forced calm into his steps as he walked over and shut his office door. Then he slumped to his knees, sucking in breaths to settle the uneven pounding of his heart. He hadn't lost his job. Michelle didn't hate him entirely. His life could go back to normal.

Except…

He still had no recollection of the day before.

That couldn't stop him from getting back to work, though. So he pushed himself up and moved to his desk. Within minutes he was in his usual groove.

#

The house was quiet when he got home. Jerry must have gone out, and Denver was glad to not have to talk to anyone. Jerry would've asked how his boys were, if Michelle had gotten herself a trophy or not. Denver didn't need that right now. What he needed was a drink and a good book.

He fell asleep surprisingly easily, and the morning started as usual. Bathroom. Coffee. Jerry sleeping in because he had work tonight. Denver grabbed the pen and leaned toward the calendar. May fourteenth still stood unmarked, and he considered putting an X there. Or should he leave it and mark the sixteenth, moving on as usual?

He paused.

What if….

He took a quick survey of the room. The microwave clock said six a.m. The t-shirt he'd slept in was the one he'd gotten on a business trip in San Diego. He was wearing his favorite pair of sweatpants.

Denver moved the pen toward the page and shifted his arm to the right. Tightening his grip and clenching his jaw, he marked Saturday, May eighteenth.

The floor lurched under Denver's feet. His head throbbed with pain. Sunlight blared into the kitchen. Not six a.m. any longer. He glanced at the microwave clock. It was almost noon.

His coffee sat on the counter, nearly in the same place it had been when he set it down the morning of May sixteenth—what he'd thought was the morning of May sixteenth. Only, now a tiny liquor bottle sat next to it.

Huh? He looked closer. Rum. He picked up the coffee and sipped, then ran to the sink and spat it out. What had he done? Why was he—

And then an old saying popped into his head: A hair of the dog that bit you.

That explained the throbbing headache. He was hungover. Massively. Yet he didn't have the memories of the night before to justify it.

A deep sigh escaped him. The throbbing in his brain eased enough for him to notice an annoying itch on his left shoulder. He reached up with his right hand to scratch, and found the skin covered with a bandage. He lifted the sleeve of his t-shirt—not the shirt from San Diego, he noticed—and started pulling at the edges of the tape, then carefully peeled the bandage off.

Inked skin lay beneath. A black tribal dragon coiled around a Celtic cross.

Of course, Jerry chose that moment to step into the kitchen.

"Whoa, dude, nice tat." He moved closer to Denver and inspected the tattoo. "That's some fine work. No wonder you were out so late. That took some serious time."

Denver leaned his weight to the side so his hip pressed against the edge of the countertop—it was the only way he could keep his balance. "Thanks," he said.

Jerry was right. The tattoo was fine work. Exactly the image Denver had been wanting for years but had been too scared to get. He admitted that to himself finally. He'd made excuses for not getting it before, albeit unvoiced to anyone but the inside of his own head, as he'd never told a soul he even wanted one.

Denver dropped the sleeve back down and gently smoothed it out. He looked at Jerry. "Why are you up? Don't you have to work tonight?"

A puzzled expression settled on Jerry's face. "I told you, I switched shifts with Brent."

"Oh, yeah, right. Sorry. I'm a bit fuzzy this morning."

Jerry looked down at the liquor bottle on the counter, one eyebrow angled up. "I bet." He cleared his throat, and then turned to make a cup of coffee. "Listen, Den, I just want you to know you don't have to..." He shot a glanced at the bottle again. "Whatever it is that's going on, I'm here."

The words hung in Jerry's ears. Whatever it is. Did Jerry not actually know? What had Denver said to him? Jerry claimed Denver had made him promise not to bring it up—a promise Jerry had, sort of, broken twice now—but had Denver not told him what "it" was? Unfortunately, there was no way to find out without asking Jerry.

Or, he could try marking May fourteenth.

Would that work? Would Denver go back and live that day, or had he already and just missed his chance to remember it?

The thunk of Jerry's coffee mug on the counter pulled him out of his thoughts.

He offered a smile. "Thanks. I know I can count on you."

Jerry nodded, bangs flipping in front of his eye. He pushed them back, then jerked his head toward the living room where two game controllers lay on the coffee table. "Let's hit Death War. Time for me to humiliate you again."

Denver laughed. "You wish."

#

Three hours later, they dragged themselves away from the couch and made sandwiches. They sat back down, and Jerry reached for his game controller. Denver set his plate on the coffee table, and grabbed the TV remote, changing the input.

Jerry groaned. "What the--?"

"Trust me," Denver said, pulling up Netflix. He started scrolling through, searching for some classic sci-fi.

When Jerry saw what Denver was doing, he settled back on the couch, sandwich plate balanced on his lap. "Whatcha got in mind?"

Denver shrugged. "Not sure. Maybe something with time travel."

The rest of the day passed in a series of movies, pizza delivery, and a shared six pack. Denver crashed into bed that night, tired but content.

The following morning, he stood in front of the calendar again. He'd slept in, and Jerry was gone already. A note lay on the counter next to his coffee mug. Headed to church early. Said I'd help out in the sound booth today since I had yesterday off. ~J

Denver held the marker in his hand. Which day should he mark off? Tempted as he was to go back to the fourteenth and try to get everything in order again, something deep inside squeezed tight at the thought. Maybe it'd all reset and he'd have no memory of skipping days. Maybe it'd jinx this whatever that was happening. He didn't want to take the chance of either. Despite the love he had for order, his curiosity overpowered that desire.

He tilted his head, considering. Yesterday, he'd woken up with a hangover and no memory of the night of drinking before. If he marked that day, he'd get to drink and not worry about suffering the hangover afterward, since he'd already done so. At the very least, the hangover would be justified for him.

Tightening his grip, he marked off Friday, May seventeenth.

#

The day started off as a typical Friday, and stayed that way until four o'clock, when Mr. Harrison called him into the conference room. Denver arrived to find Mr. Harrison and Michelle sitting at the far end of the long, polished wood table. Three bottles of water sat on coasters in front of the chairs they occupied and a third, empty one. Denver took his seat. Neither of his superiors offered a hand shake, so

Denver grabbed his water and twisted the bottle cap.

"Good afternoon," he said as calmly as he could with his heart thudding time and a half.

Why had he been called in? Michelle had said on Wednesday that the work he'd done on the Toch Industries account had been excellent. She seemed to have completely forgiven him for the day he'd missed. Of course, Thursday was still a blank at this point, so he could have screwed up again. Or they could have found something wrong they hadn't noticed before.

Mr. Harrison tapped the table with his index finger. "Denver, you know we were pleased with the work you did, despite the day you missed. And had we known you were sick in bed all day with food poisoning…well."

Denver did all he could to keep surprise from registering on his face. He had no memory of the Tuesday he'd missed, but everything from Wednesday said food poisoning had not been a part of it. There'd been no evidence of anyone puking or otherwise in his bathroom. But more importantly, he knew he'd been to give blood on Tuesday, which meant he'd been fine in the morning. Unless his breakfast of oatmeal—the only thing he ever ate for breakfast, if he ate at all—had given him food poisoning, it would've had to have been something he ate at lunch, which meant he'd have gone to work and turned in the files.

He shot a glance at Michelle. She just nodded.

Denver looked back at Mr. Harrison. "Thank you, sir."

Mr. Harrison waved his hand as if dismissing the thanks. "The point is, you've been doing an outstanding job all around. And we think you'd be perfect for the supervisor position in the new department."

There was no stopping the surprise from filling his expression this time. Nor the grin that spread across his face. "Sir, I don't know what to say." He laughed. "I mean, yes, of course. Yes, I want the position. Very much so."

Mr. Harrison stood and extended his arm. Denver followed suit, clasping his boss's hand in a firm shake. "Glad to hear it," Mr. Harrison said, and then he nodded at Michelle and left the room.

Michelle leaned back in her seat and crossed her arms. "I say it's a night for celebrating. How about we grab the rest of the team and knock off early? We can make it to Neagan's in time for happy hour."

Neagan's Pub was right next to a tattoo parlor. Denver rubbed is shoulder, the skin underneath his shirt as yet uninked. "Sounds perfect."

#

The next day Denver marked was Thursday, May sixteenth. He wanted at least that gap filled, although he would not allow his marker to touch May fourteenth, just in case. The sixteenth would be the last day he had to live working his old position. Best to get it over with, then it would be all new days in a new job ahead.

It was a typical Thursday. The only thing at all odd—or what would have been odd had he not already lived Friday—was Michelle stopping in to tell him she'd covered for him. "Mr. Harrison thinks you were out with food poisoning on Tuesday," she said. "You're welcome." That was it; she left his office without giving him a chance to reply.

He'd already skipped Sunday once, and decided that after Thursday he'd leave it for later again. He struggled with the urge to live the first week of his new job in order but couldn't pass up the opportunity to have a first day that didn't feel like a first day, and jumped ahead to the following Thursday, May twenty-third.

It was brilliant. He was already getting the hang of things, so when he jumped back to Monday—after living Wednesday, then Friday, then Tuesday—he marched in on his "first" day and wowed everyone. Not to mention putting Monday at the end of the week made it feel like Friday, so his mood couldn't have been better.

Until his assistant walked into his office after lunch. Beth smiled sweetly at him as she stood on the other side of the desk. "You got a call while you were out, Mr. Barret. I took a message." She handed him a piece of paper that detailed the call. Marjory from the blood bank had called, wanting to make sure Denver was doing well after "his experience" on the fourteenth.

Beth continued, "She said the number they had for you didn't work last week, and by the time they tracked down your work number, you'd been moved over here. I told her you seemed to be doing just fine, but she hoped you'd call her back so she could be sure."

Denver stared at the note. "Thank you, Beth." He lifted his gaze to find her looking concerned. He smiled reassuringly. "I just got a bit woozy the last time I gave blood."

"And they called to check on you. That's very sweet."

"I've been going there a long time. Just hit the three gallon mark."

Beth's smile widened. "How wonderful of you. You're saving lives." She took a step backward. "Well, I need to get back to it. Glad you're feeling better."

After she left his office, Denver crumpled the note and threw it in the trash. Something had happened that day, something that had Marjory worried about him, and it was definitely not just him getting a little woozy. He could call her back and find out. Should call her back so she wouldn't worry. But that thing deep inside tightened again, as it had the day he'd almost marked off the fourteenth. Something was telling him he didn't want to know. He surely didn't want to find out over the phone with Marjory. When the time came, if the time came, he'd find out with a neat little X over the number fourteen.

#

Denver used the skipped Sunday to give himself a three-day weekend. Jerry came home from church whistling something that was no doubt a song they'd played in the service that day. "You missed a good one," he said to Denver as he opened the fridge for a glass of grape juice. "Nothing like rockin' the house of God."

"Glad you had a good time," Denver said. Jerry had invited him to church several times, but Denver just had no interest. The song Jerry was whistling was catchy, but that wasn't enough to get Denver to want anything to do with organized religion. Not to mention, he had a hard time believing the other members of Jerry's church were as genuine as Jerry. People, no matter what their beliefs, generally weren't. Eventually, Jerry quit asking Denver, but he always came home on Sundays...well, the only word that fit was stoked. And for Denver this weekend had two Sundays, which meant a double-shot of stoked Jerry. He reminded himself to space out his Sundays next time.

Over the next few weeks, it became a game for Denver. Figuring out which days to live in which order. Working to keep the details straight. Following conversations about things that had happened on the days he skipped, and silent smiles when he went back to those days knowing what would be said about everything in the future. It was fun, if a bit maddening at times. More than once, Denver had to make notes to himself, and at one point he pondered creating a flow chart to track everything.

To keep it from not getting too confusing, he didn't jump far ahead, clustering the out-of-order days in groups no longer than a week. Then, one morning he found himself staring at the calendar. Every day in May except the fourteenth was filled in. The first three weeks of June had been filled in as well.

He flipped to July, wondering how much longer he should continue. At some point the game would get old. At some point he would likely want to start living day-to-day again. Maybe it was time to get a little wilder before giving this up.

The page open to July, Denver went straight to the thirty-first.

The marker pushed away from the page, like a magnet being repelled by another. A strong magnet. He tried marking a few days before, and the same thing happened.

Maybe he could only jump ahead so far?

It was probably for the best.

With a sigh, he dropped the page back down, and marked June twenty-fourth. Which turned out to be a high-stress Monday at work, leaving him exhausted and irritable when he got home. Jerry had already left for his night shift, so at least the house was quiet.

Denver flipped on the news, tossed the remote onto the coffee table, then walked into the kitchen and grabbed a beer from the fridge.

As he passed the barstool on his way back into the living room, he noticed the pile of mail on the upholstered seat.

Setting his beer on the counter, he squinted at the envelope on top. It was addressed to him. The return address was for Memorial Hospital. Both addresses were visible through clear plastic windows that showed enough to make it obvious the envelope contained a bill.

So, he'd been to the hospital. And it had to have been on May fourteenth, as that was the only day left unmarked through today.

Denver could open it. Maybe it wouldn't say explicitly what had happened to him, but it would have some information. The details of the bill would give him clues. It could contain the charge for an ambulance ride, or laboratory tests. It may say what kind of doctor he'd seen.

Or doctors, plural.

His heart stuttered and his throat suddenly felt smaller, tight and dry.

Then a thought pushed through the panic: No symptoms. He'd experienced nothing over the past few weeks. No pain, no dizziness.

No puking. Not even a cold. Surely whatever had taken him to the hospital had turned out to be nothing. If not so, he'd have gotten sent to see a specialist or something, right?

His heartrate steadied, and he took a gulp of beer, noting that his throat felt back to normal. It was all going to be fine.

After the news, Denver tossed his empty beer bottles into the recycle bin. On his way out of the kitchen, he snatched the hospital bill from the barstool seat, then ripped it into pieces as he walked to his bedroom and dumped it all into the trashcan in his bathroom.

#

Denver finished up the month of June and flipped over to July. Again he impulsively moved his hand to July thirty-first, and again the marker was repelled by an unseen force. He back-tracked as he'd done before, but none of the spaces after the thirteenth would allow him to mark their numbers. He held the marker over the thirteenth, and did not feel the repelling force, but he didn't X out the number.

Two weeks, then, must be as far as the calendar would let him go forward from the last marked day. He shrugged and put an X over July fifth. Might as well get his post-Fourth of July hangover out of the way.

The first week of July—Friday, Tuesday, Monday, Saturday, Thursday, Wednesday, Sunday—sped by. His new job had reached a point of comfort. He and Michelle still worked together quite a bit, but as equals now. The raise that had come with the promotion had meant he could pay his car off. He could buy a new phone, maybe a better laptop. And get some new clothes. He went shopping on Friday after work, for the first time not worrying about the cost. New work shirts, new dress pants, a pair of shoes that didn't dig into his toe. And a leather jacket he'd been eyeing that had gone on sale, making it, with his new pay level, barely affordable.

As he hung everything in his closet on Tuesday, he yanked down old clothes he'd been wanting to get rid of, including the pants he'd worn on May fourteenth. He only knew he'd worn them that day because he found them in the hamper when he'd done his laundry later that week. He hadn't worn them since. He hadn't worn any of the clothes from the fourteenth, including his new blood donation milestone shirt. Denver folded the old clothes and put them into a bag for donation, going through the pockets first to make sure he hadn't left anything of value in them, even though he normally checked everything as he loaded it into the washer. Of course, he found nothing until he stuck his hand into the May fourteenth pants pockets. He remembered throwing them into the machine without checking, at the time almost afraid of touching them. Now, he found a wadded up piece of paper, softened into a ball from going through the washer and dryer.

His throat tightened. There was something about the paper. He had no idea what, no memory still of that day, only a feeling of dread he couldn't explain. He did not want to see that paper. Yet, he found himself dropping the pants onto the bed and carefully prying at the paper wad. Much of it was gunked together, and some of it crumbled apart. But one corner pulled away. All Denver could make out were three words as he smoothed it out, each with letters smudged or washed off: Against Medical Advice.

The doctor had wanted him to stay. But Denver had left anyway. Signed a form, ignored the doctor's advice. Denver, who had never missed a cleaning at the dentist, never missed an annual physical, had gone to every follow-up appointment he'd ever had. Not that there had been that many. He'd been healthy overall but had the typical stuff. Stomach flu, weird rash that one time after camping, broken arm when he fell off the top of his truck at a tailgate party back in college. He'd never failed to finish a course of antibiotics. He would never walk out of a hospital against a doctor's advice.

But he had. Why?

The only reason he could imagine was that it must have been something horrible. Something he couldn't deal with. Something that scared him.

Something that made it pointless to stay. Either because he thought the doctor was overreacting…or because it was something so awful Denver couldn't handle it.

Denver wadded the paper back up and tossed it into the garbage. Either it was nothing to worry about, or it was something he'd face eventually, if and when he chose to mark May fourteenth. Maybe he would never have to make that choice.

On Monday, Jerry got a promotion at his company as well, and a raise, and celebrated by buying a TV that barely fit the entertainment center. The first time they used it while playing video games, Jerry let out a hoot of joy, and every five minutes he exclaimed, "Check out those graphics, Den!" Of course, Denver had already experienced the TV on Friday and Tuesday and missed the opportunity to appreciate Jerry's enthusiasm along with him.

After he'd marked Saturday and Thursday, Denver began to think it would be time very soon to start marking days in order again.

Things were good in order. Going to work on Tuesday after having splurged on clothes Friday, thus not having them yet to wear, was frustrating. More so on Thursday after skipping ahead to Saturday—back to work sans the new phone he'd picked up.

Yet, when he hit the end of the first week, Denver couldn't help trying the days later in July. The month had Xes on July first through seventh. He aimed the marker at July seventeenth, but it was pushed away.

The two-week theory was apparently wrong.

The sixteenth refused an X as well.

Then the fifteenth.

Fourteenth.

As before, he felt no resistance when he held the marker over July thirteenth.
Why?

He moved his hand to the right again and pushed toward the calendar page with all his might. The harder he pushed, the harder the unseen force pushed back. But he forced more energy to his muscles.

The marker moved forward a fraction of an inch.

The calendar blurred, the numbers fading.

Blackness closed in around Denver. Cold, empty.

The room disappeared from his vision. He felt no floor beneath his feet, no countertop against his side. He felt nothing but the marker in his hand, although even his hand felt separated from him.

He wasn't breathing.

He wasn't…anything.

He dropped the marker.

Air rushed into his lungs, and he gulped it down, gripping the edge of the counter. His heart pounded against his ribs. Ribs that he felt now, ribs that were definitely a part of him at this moment but had definitely not been a moment ago.

Denver looked up at the calendar.

The days stopped at July thirteenth—after that, the page was blank.

Jerry appeared in the doorway to the kitchen, hair a tangled mess and eyes bleary. It was still Monday—Denver hadn't marked the calendar yet, so the day had just gone to the next open square, July eighth—and Jerry was sleeping in because he had work that night.

"Den, what the heck?"

Denver inhaled and forced himself to stand up straight. "What?"

"That noise you made. I thought you fell or something." He yawned and rubbed the back of his neck.

"No, I'm fine. Sorry I woke you."

"No worries. But you don't look so great. This," he said, waving his hand up and down, indicating Denver's appearance, "is where they came up with the saying 'death warmed over.'"

Denver swallowed and forced out a sarcastic, "Thanks."

"Any time." Jerry turned and plodded back toward his room. A moment later, his voice rang from the hall. "Maybe you ought to call in sick today, dude." Then a few more footsteps and the thud of his bedroom door shutting.

Denver ignored Jerry's suggestion, honing in on the words he'd said before. What noise had Denver made? Did Denver really look that bad?

He shuffled to his bathroom and looked in the mirror. Jerry was right. Denver had never looked so pale. Dark gray rimmed his eyes. And if he hadn't thought it was completely crazy, he'd have sworn the edges of his lips looked blue.

Death warmed over.

He'd felt dead.

Maybe he had been.

He returned to the calendar—blank past July thirteenth—and called out, "Jerry!"

Seconds passed while Denver stared at the half-printed, half-blank page, and then Jerry appeared in the doorway of the kitchen again.

"Dude, what gives? I gotta work tonight."

"I'm sorry. And…I know this is going to sound crazy but look at the calendar."

Jerry shuffled around and made an exaggerated *I'm looking* expression. "Yeah, what?"

"Nothing weird?" Denver said, unable to keep the hesitation from his voice.

"Well, you forgot to write my mom's birthday on here, but that's it."

"You're sure?"

Jerry turned to face him, his eyes filled with concern. "For real, dude. Call in. Get some rest." He patted Denver on the shoulder. "Stay home, and I'll check on ya before I head to work."

Denver nodded and let Jerry move past him. Maybe he did need to take a day off. He marked July eighth on the calendar and went to find his cell phone.

#

Sleeping in, reading, and watching TV had made a world of difference in the way Denver felt, but it hadn't cleared the thoughts that plagued him. Why could he not mark anything past the thirteenth of July? Did it have to do with not marking the fourteenth? Could he only go so far from that day without going back?

Or was it worse? What had really happened on the fourteenth? Had the doctor given him some kind of med that had a delayed side-effect, like a causing a blood clot that would release on the thirteenth and cause a massive stroke, making it his last day? Or maybe he was going to die anyway on that day, but it had nothing to do with his trip to the hospital. Maybe he was destined to be hit by a bus or crack his skull on the coffee table after tripping over Jerry's shoes or have a heart attack. Maybe his ex-girlfriend was going to go mental and shoot him at work. Maybe he'd be in a horrible car accident.

He stood staring at the half-blank page again on the morning of July ninth. For a brief moment, he'd tried holding the marker over the white expanse on the bottom of the page, but nothing appeared, and Denver felt as though his body were lightening. As though the atoms were disconnecting from each other the way he'd imagined it would feel on the transporter pad of the Enterprise.

It could only mean one thing. His life would end on July thirteenth. The reason he couldn't mark days beyond that, and the reason he could no longer see those days at all was there were no days for him past that point. Jerry could see them because Jerry wasn't going to die yet.

Denver, on the other hand, would die in four days. It was the only explanation. If he merely had to return to May fourteenth, surely the rest of the calendar would not have gone blank. Right?

He reached up and pulled down the two calendar pages that would take him back to May. With a deep breath, he held the marker a few inches away from May fourteenth. His hand hovered for a moment, and he moved it forward. There was no resistance as there were with the days following July thirteenth, but his stomach turned and bile crept up the back of his throat. Dread washed over him, although he didn't know if it was the power of the calendar or just his own fear of finding out the truth.

The marker moved forward until it touched the page. Denver's hand shook as the room swam around him. Panic seized him and stuttered his heartbeats. His vision darkened, blackness moving inward until only a pinprick remained in the center. The pinprick grew, spreading out in all directions at once, filling with different hues that swirled and morphed into shapes. Moving shapes that tightened and clarified just enough to be discernible.

The blood donation center, in the waiting room. Marjory walking over and handing him a clipboard. Half paying attention, half looking at his emails and texts on his phone.

Distracted, scribbling down the wrong phone number.

Then in the donation room, rising from his seat, bandaid already in place. The room spins and slips from view.

Motion and blur and sirens.

A bright hallway and ceiling tiles whizzing past.

Doctors, nurses, beeping machines.

Metal table, sliding into a human-sized tube, clicks and whirs and banging noises. A voice reminding him to hold still.

Sitting up but looking down at the purple shirt covering his torso, white dress shirt wadded in his hands, fingers fumbling the frayed tear on the sleeve. A voice murmuring, the only word clear enough to understand—*inoperable*—rebounding around his brain.

Scrawling his signature on a form, shoving it into his pants pocket, letting the heavy door slam shut behind him.

Ripping off the bandaid and wristband and tossing them, along with the torn work shirt, into the trashcan on the sidewalk. Hailing a cab. Picking up his car and driving home. Sitting in the car, scrolling through internet searches—*brain aneurysm, inoperable, prognosis*—on his phone.

Walking into the house. Jerry home early, eyes filled with worry.

"Where've you been? What's going on?"

"Nowhere. Don't ask. Don't ever ask."

"But—"

"Swear it!"

"I'll pray for you."

"Whatever."

Lying in bed, staring out the window. Scared. Helpless. Hopeless…

Blackness circled the vision and drew inward until, again, only a pinprick of light remained, and then popped.

Denver stood in the same spot, arm up, the tip of the marker touching May fourteenth. Before he could decide what to do, before he could decide what to think, an X appeared over the square. Perfect, straight lines from corner to corner. Perfect angles. Red, the color of blood.

He dropped the marker, ran to the kitchen sink, and vomited. His stomach clenched tighter with each heave until he slumped over the edge of the sink, willing Jerry to not hear, to stay in his room. Sweat clung to his face, his chest, the back of his neck. The sight inside the sink threatened to start the process again, so he rinsed it out and splashed cold water on his face.

Several deep breaths, and his heartbeat settled. He swallowed hard, forcing himself to turn around. It was his imagination, surely.

But when he returned to the calendar, the red X was there.

Jaw clenched, he lifted the pages and fastened them in place so July showed again. Eight neat black Xes covered the first eight days. He held the marker over the number nine. There was no more reason to jump. The last four days of your life were the last four days regardless of what order they came in.

Four days left, all because of May fourteenth.

The day he'd first marked the wrong number on the calendar.

The day he'd gone in to give blood and ended up at the hospital, to be billed for weeks later.

The day he'd signed an "Against Medical Advice" form and stormed out.

The day he'd told Jerry something bad had happened but never revealed that thing to his friend.

The day not just the order of time changed for Denver, but the way he looked at life.

He rubbed at the fully healed tattoo on his shoulder and glanced at the huge TV. He thought about the new wardrobe in his closet. The phone, the laptop. Promotions, raises. He thought about days of video games, movies, and beer. A friendship with Jerry that had deepened. The fun he'd had making a game of the shifting days.

Would those things have happened if he'd remembered?

He marked July ninth.

The following day, he marked Wednesday, July tenth.

Thursday, eleventh.

Friday, twelfth.

#

He talked Jerry into switching shifts on Friday so he'd have the day off. They spent the day together, renting jet skis at the lake. Denver took Jerry out to his favorite sushi place for dinner, and even choked down a sip of saki at Jerry's insistence. The rest of the evening consisted of video games and a six pack of Denver's favorite porter.

At the end of the night, Jerry thanked him after downing a glass of water before bed. Denver sat in one of the barstools, staring at the calendar.

One more day.

The end of this life, and then...what? The nothingness he'd felt before when he'd tried to mark the calendar beyond the thirteenth squirmed in the back of his mind. So cold, so empty. So wrong. The sensation screamed of *lacking*, of should be, as though it could and would be *something*, if only—

The clink of Jerry's glass in the sink drew his attention. Jerry stood, arms now crossed, lip tucked between his teeth.

Denver's throat burned and tightened, but he clasped his hands together and forced out the words he never thought he'd hear himself say. "Jerry…um…would you pray for me?"

Jerry's gaze intensified, and he nodded, no questions asked. Then he walked over and stood behind Denver, placing his hands on Denver's shoulders. Denver closed his eyes, listening to Jerry's voice. "Dear Lord…"

Denver didn't really hear Jerry's prayer. He focused on holding back the tears that burned his eyes. It didn't matter what Jerry said anyway—it only mattered that he was saying it.

#

And now, the calendar hangs in front of him. Every square visible to Denver marked with a perfect little X, except for July thirteenth. Denver picks up the marker from the where it lies on the counter. He inhales, pulling his shoulders back, and marks the day.

The End

Kat Heckenbach

Kat grew up in a small town, where she spent most of her time either drawing or sitting in her "reading tree" with her nose buried in a fantasy novel...except for the hours pretending her back yard was an enchanted forest that could only be reached through the secret passage in her closet. She never could give up on the idea that maybe she really was magic, mistakenly placed in a world not her own--but as the years past, and no elves or fairies carted her away, she realized she was just going to have to create the life of her fantasies with words. Her characters always find a secret world--whether it be real, imaginary, or in the pages of a book. Find out more at: http://www.katheckenbach.com/

Publisher Information

Find out more at: www.bearpublications.com

Printed in the USA
CPSIA information can be obtained
at www.ICGtesting.com
LVHW091324191023
761544LV00001B/61

9 781643 706689